WORDS WITHOUT PICTURES

Words by
Alan Moore
Neil Gaiman
Jon J Muth
Ann Nocenti
Mark Evanier
Charles Vess
Stephen R. Bissette

Faces by
John Bolton

Edited by
Stephen Niles

Arcane/Eclipse

Entire Contents © 1990 Arcane Books and Eclipse Books;
The Hypothetical Lizard © 1990 Alan Moore; *Foreign Parts*
© 1990 Neil Gaiman; *Four Poems* © 1990 Jon J Muth;
A Shot of Damns and a Pack of Hells © 1990 Ann Nocenti;
A Creature Most Dreadful © 1990 Mark Evanier;
*A Short Tale of a Young Man Who Would
Have Been a Priest* © 1990 Charles Vess;
*Jiz and Blood: Everything Merges With
the Night* © 1990 Stephen R. Bissette;
Introduction © 1990 Matt Feazell;
caricatures © 1990 John Bolton.

A previous, illustrated form of
*A Short Tale of a Young Man Who
Would Have Been a Priest*
appeared in *Eclipse Magazine*.

Book design: Kathy Cashel
Cover design: Mark Cox

Produced by Arcane Books for
Eclipse Books
P. O.Box 1099
Forestville, California 95436

Cloth: ISBN 1-56060-031-4
Paper: ISBN 1-56060-032-2

First printing

CONTENTS

Introduction
   By Matt Feazell iii
The Hypothetical Lizard
   By Alan Moore 1
Foreign Parts
   By Neil Gaiman 73
Four Poems
   By Jon J Muth 105
A Shot of Damns and a Pack of Hells
   By Ann Nocenti 117
A Creature Most Dreadful
   By Mark Evanier 129
A Short Tale of a Young Man
   Who Would Have Been a Priest
   By Charless Vess 151
Jiz and Blood: Everything Merges
   With the Night
   By Stephen R. Bissette 161

A SPECIAL INTRODUCTION

By Matt Feazel

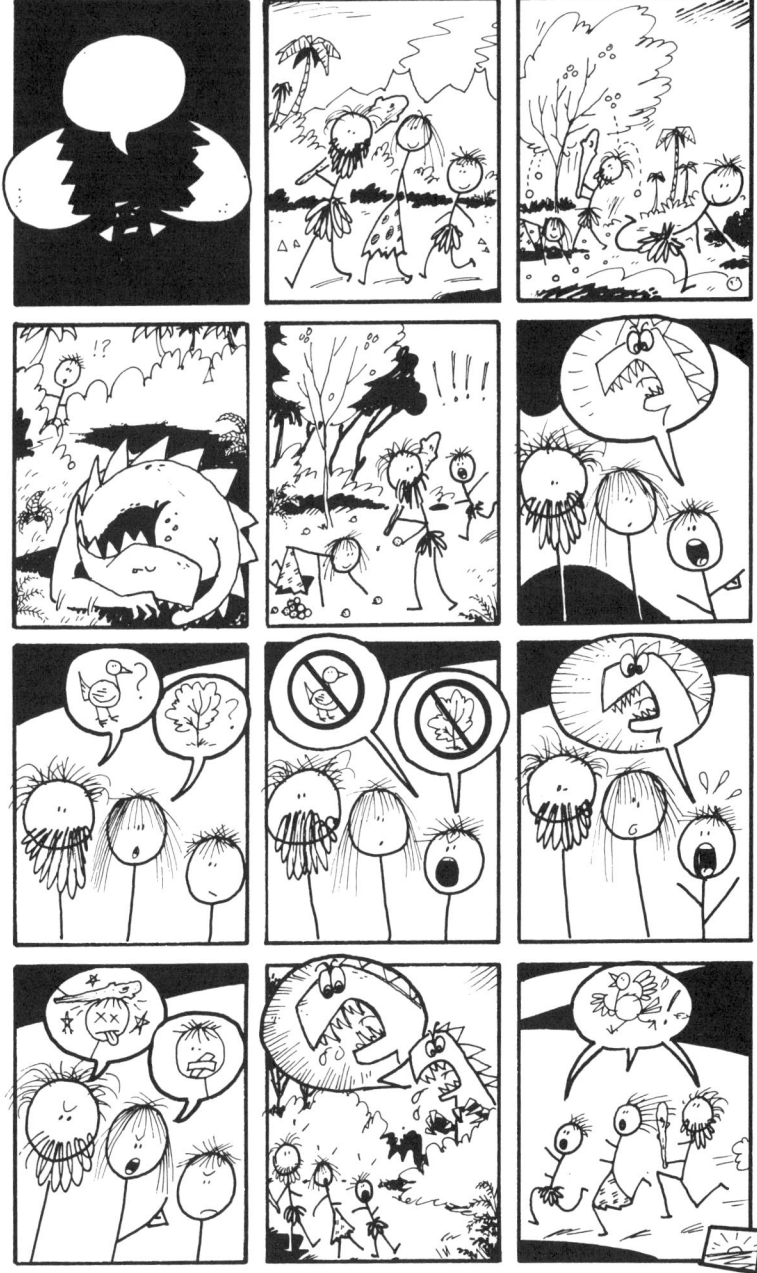

THE
HYPOTHETICAL
LIZARD

By Alan Moore

HALF HER FACE was porcelain.

Seated upon her balcony, absently chewing the anemic blue flowers she had plucked from her window garden, Som-Som regarded the courtyard of the House Without Clocks. Unadorned and circular, it lay beneath her like a shadowy and stagnant well. The black flagstones, polished to an impassive luster by the passage of many feet, looked more like still water than stone when viewed from above. The cracks and fissures that might have spoiled the effect were visible only where veins of moss followed their winding seams through the otherwise featureless jet. It could as easily have been a delicate lattice of pond scum that would shatter and disperse with the first splash, the first ripple...

When Som-Som was five her mother had noticed the aching beauty prefigured in her infant face and had brought the uncomprehending child through the yammering maze of nighttime Liavek until they reached the pastel house with its round black courtyard. Yielding to the tug of her mother's hand, Som-Som dragged across the midnight slabs with the echo of her shuffling footsteps whispering back to her from the high, curved wall that bounded all but a quarter of the enclosure. The concave facade of the House Without Clocks itself completed the circle, and into its broad arc were set seven doors, each of a different color. It was at the central door, the white one, that her mother knocked.

There was the sound of small and careful footsteps, followed by the brief muttering of a latch as the door was unlocked from the other side. It glided noiselessly open. Dressed all in white against the whiteness of the chambers beyond, a fifteen-year-old girl stared out into the dark at them, her eyes remote and unquestioning. The garment she wore was shaped to her body and colored like snow, with faint blue shadows pooling in its folds and creases. It covered her from head to toe, save for the openings that had been cut away to reveal her right breast, her left hand, and her impenetrable masklike face.

Staring up at the slim figure framed in its icy rectangle of light, Som-Som had at first assumed that the girl's visible flesh was reddened by the application of paint or powder. Looking closer, she realized with a thrill of fascination and horror that the skin was entirely covered by small yet legible words, tattooed in vivid crimson upon the smooth white canvas beneath. Finely worded sentences, ambiguous and suggestive, spiraled out from the maroon bud of her nipple. Verses of elegant and cryptic passion followed the orbit of her left eye before resolving themselves into a perfect metaphor beneath the shadow of her cheekbone. Her fingers dripped with poetry.

She looked first at Som-Som and then at her mother, and there was no judgement in her eyes. As if something had been agreed upon, she turned and walked with tiny, precise steps into the arctic dazzle of the House Without Clocks. After an instant, Som-Som and her mother followed, closing the white door behind them.

The girl (whose name, Som-Som later learned, was Book) led the two of them through spectrally perfumed corridors to a room that was at once gigantic and blinding. White light, refracted through lenses and faceted glassware, seemed to hang in the air like a ghostly cobweb, so that the shapes and forms within the room were softened. At the center of this foggy phosphorescence, a tall woman reclined upon polar furs, the cushions strewn about her feet embossed with intricate frost patterns. The glimmering blur of her surroundings erased the wrinkles from her skin and made her ageless, but when she spoke her voice was old. Her name was Ouish, and she was the mistress and proprietor of the House Without Clocks.

The conversation that passed between the two women was low and obscure, and Som-Som caught little of it. At one point, Mistress Ouish rose from her bed of white pelts and hobbled across to inspect the child. The old woman had taken Som-Som's face lightly between thumb and forefinger, turning the head in order to study the profile. Her touch was like crepe, but surprisingly warm in a room that gleamed with such unearthly coldness. Evidently satisfied, she turned and nodded once to the girl called Book before returning to the embrace of the furs.

The tattooed servant left the room, returning some moments later bearing a small pouch of bleached leather. It jingled faintly as she walked. She handed it to Som-Som's mother, who looked frightened and uncertain. Its weight seemed to reassure her, and she did not resist or complain as Book took her lightly by the arm and guided her out of the white chamber. Long minutes passed before Som-Som realized that her mother was not coming back.

There was Khafi, a nineteen-year-old dislocationist who, lying upon his stomach, could curl his body backward until the buttocks were seated comfortably upon the top of his head while his face smiled out from between the ankles. There was Delice, a woman in middle age who used fourteen needles to provoke inconceivable pleasures and torments, all without leaving the faintest mark. Mopetel, suspending her own heartbeat and breath, could approximate a corpse-like state for more than two hours. Jazu had fine black hair growing all over his body and would walk upon all fours and only communicate in growls. And there was Rushushi, and Hata, and unblinking Loba Pak...

Living amidst this menagerie of exotics, where the singular was worn down by repeated contact until it became the commonplace, Som-Som was afforded a certain objectivity. Without discrimination or favor, she spent the best part of her days observing the animate rarities about her, wondering which of them provided a template for what she was to become. Eavesdropping upon Mistress Ouish and her closest associates, patiently decoding their under-language of pauses and accentuated syllables, Som-Som had determined that she was being preserved for something special. special even amid the gallery of specialties that was the House Without Clocks. Would she be instructed in the art of driving men and women to ecstasy with the vibrations of her voice, like Hata? Would Mopetel's talent of impermanent death become hers? Smiling as she accepted the candied fruits and marzipans offered by her indulgent elders, she would study their faces and consider.

Upon her ninth birthday, Som-Som was escorted by Book to the dazzling sanctum of Mistress Ouish. Her parched smile disquieting with its uncharacteristic warmth, Mistress Ouish had dismissed Book and then patted the wintery hides beside her, gesturing for Som-Som to sit. With what looked like someone else's expression stitched across her face, the proprietor fo the House Without Clocks informed Som-Som of what might be her unique position within that establishment.

If she wished, she would become a whore of sorcerers, exclusive to their use. Henceforth, only those cunning hands that sculpted fortune itself would have access to the warm slopes of her substance. She would come to understand the abstracted lusts of those who moved the secret levers of the world, and she would be happy in their service.

Kneeling at the very edge of the bed of silver fur, Som-Som had felt the world shudder to a standstill as the old woman's words rolled about inside her head, crashing together like huge glass planets.

Sorcerers?

Often, sent to fetch some minor philter or remedy for the older inhabitants of the House Without Clocks, Som-Som's errands had taken her to Wizard's Row. The street, itself, shifting and inconstant, full of small movements at the periphery of the vision, presented no clear and consistent image that she could summon from her memory. Some of its denizens, however, were unforgettable. Their eyes. Their terrible, knowing eyes...

She pictured herself naked before a gaze that had known the depths of the oceans of chance in which people are but fishes, a gaze that saw the secret wave-patterns in those unfathomable tides of circumstance. In her stomach, something more ambiguous than either fear or exhilaration began to extend its tendrils. Somewhere far away, in a white room filled with obscuring brilliance, Mistress Ouish was detailing a list of those conditions that must be fulfilled before Som-Som could commence her new duties.

Firstly, it seemed that many who dealt in the manipulation of luck would themselves leave nothing to chance. Before such a sorcerer would enter fully into physical congress with another being, the inflexible observation of certain precautions was demanded. Foremost amongst these were those safeguards pertaining to secrecy. The ecstasies of wizards were events of awesome and terrifying moment, during which their power was at its most capricious, its least contained.

It was not unknown for various phenomena to manifest spontaneously, or for the name of a luck-invested object to be murmured at the moment of release. In the world of the magicians, such indiscretions could be of lethal consequence. The most innocent of boudoir confidences, if relayed to an enemy of sufficient ruthlessness, might yield a dreadful harvest for the incautious thaumaturge. Perhaps he would be plucked from the nigh by cold hands with unblinking yellow eyes set into their palms, or perhaps a sore upon his neck would blossom into purple, babyish lips, whispering delirious obscenities into his ear until all reason was driven from him.

The intangible continent of fortune was a territory steeped in hazard, and she who would be the whore of sorcerers must also undertake to be the bride of Silence.

To this end, Som-Som would be taken to a specific residence in Wizard's Row, an address remarkable in that it could only be located upon the third and fifth days of the week. Here, the child would be given a small pickled worm, ocher in color, revealing the grayish pink mansion of her soul to the fingers of one who abided in that place, a physiomancer of great renown. At this juncture, the Silencing would commence.

Connecting the brain's hemispheres there existed a single gristly thread, the thoroughfare by which the urgent neural messages of the preverbal and intuitive right lobe might pass to its more rational and active counterpart upon the left. In Som-Som, this delicate bridge would be destroyed, severed by a sharp knife so as to permit no further communication between the two halves of the child's psyche.

Following her recovery from this surgery, the girl would be granted a year in which to adjust to her new perceptions. She would learn to balance and to pick up objects without the benefit of stereoscopic sight or depth of vision. After many bouts of tearful and frustrating paralysis, during which she would merely stand and tremble, making poignant half-completed gestures while her body remained torn between conflicting urges, she would finally achieve some measure of coordination and restored grace. Certainly, her movements would always possess a slow and slightly staggered quality, but if directed properly there was no reason why this dreamlike effect should not in itself be erotically enhancing. At the end of her year of readjustment, Som-Som would have a cast taken of her face, after which she would be fitted with the Broken Mask.

The Broken Mask was not so much broken as sliced cleanly in two. Made of porcelain and covering the entire head, it would be precisely bisected with a small, silver chisel, starting at the nape of the neck, traversing the cold and hairless cranium, descending the ridge of the nose to divide the expressionless lips forever. The left side of the mask would be taken away and crushed to a fine talcum before being thrown to the winds.

Prior to the fitting of the Broken Mask, Som-Som's head would be completely shaven, the scalp afterward rubbed with the foul-smelling mauve juices of a berry known to destroy the follicles of the hair so that there could be no regrowth. This would at least partially ensure her comfort during the next fifteen years, in which time the mask was not to be removed unless the slowly changing shape of the skull made it uncomfortable. In this eventuality, the mask would be taken from her head and recast.

Covering the right side of her head, the flawless topography of the Broken Mask would be uninterrupted by any aperture for hearing or vision. The porcelain eye was opaque and white and blind. The porcelain ear heard nothing. Concealed beneath this shell, their organic counterparts would be similarly disadvantaged. Som-Som would see nothing with her right eye, and would be deaf in her right ear. Only in the uncovered half of her face would the perceptions be unimpaired.

By some paradoxical mirror-fluke of nature, those sensory impressions gleaned from the apparatus of the body's left side would be conveyed to the brain's right hemisphere. And there, due to the severing of the neural causeway that had connected both lobes, the information would remain. It would never reach those centers of cerebral activity that govern speech and communication, for they were situated in the left brain, a land now irretrievably lost beyond the surgically created chasm. Her eye would see, but her lips would know nothing of it. Conversation that her ear might gather would forever go unrepeated by a tongue ignorant of words it should shape.

She would be blinded, but not exactly. Her hearing would remain, after a fashion, and she would even be able to speak. But she would be Silenced.

Within the flattering opalescence of her white chamber, Mistress Ouish concluded her descriptions of the honors which awaited the stunned nine-year-old. She rang the tiny china bell that signaled Book to the room, terminating the audience. Stumbling over feet made suddenly too large by loss of circulation, Som-Som allowed the tattooed servant to lead her into the startling mundane daylight.

Poised upon the threshold, Book had turned to the blinking child beside her and smiled. It wrinkled the words written upon her cheeks, rendering them briefly illegible, and it was not a cruel smile.

"When you are Silenced and can reveal their conclusions to no one, I shall permit you to read all of my stories."

Her voice was uneven of pitch, as if she had long been unpracticed in its application. Raising her ungloved and crimson-speckled hand she touched the calligraphy upon her forehead, and then, lowering it, lightly brushed the lyric spiral of her breast. Smiling once more, she turned and went inside the house, closing the white door behind her, an ambulatory pornography.

It was the first time that Som-Som had even heard her speak.

The following day, Som-Som was escorted to an elusive residence where a man with a comb of white hair that had been varnished into a stiff dorsal fin running back across his skull gave her a tiny, brownish worm to chew. She noted that it was withered and ugly, but probably no more so than it had been in life. She placed it upon her tongue, because that was expected of her, and she began to chew.

She awoke as two separate people, unspeaking strangers who shared the same skin without collaboration or conference. She was conveyed back to the House Without Clocks in a small cart lined with cushions. She rattled through the arched entranceway and across the gargantuan inkblot of the courtyard, and all that had been promised eventually came to pass.

Twelve years ago.

Seated upon her balcony, her half-visible lips stained blue by the juices of the masticated blossoms, Som-Som regarded the courtyard of the House Without Clocks. Unrippled by the afternoon breeze, the black pond stared back at her. Here and there upon the impenetrably dark water, fallen leaves were floating, motionless scraps of sepia against the blackness.

Surely, if she were to topple forward with delicious slowness toward the midnight well beneath her, surely she would come to no harm? Dropping like a pebble, she would splash through the impassive jet of the surface, a tumbling commotion of silver in the cold, ebony waters surrounding her.

Up above, the ripples would race outward like pulses of agony throbbing from a wound. They would break in black, lapping wavelets against the courtyard walls of the House Without Clocks, and then the waters would once more become as still as stone.

Down below, kicking out with clean, unfaltering strokes, she would swim beneath the ground, out below the curved walls of the House Without Clocks, out under the City of Luck itself and into those unchartered, solid oceans that lay beyond. Diving deep, she would glide among the glittering veins of ore, through the buried and forgotten strata. Darting upward, she would flicker and twist through the warm shallows of the topsoil, surfacing occasionally to leap in a shimmering arc through the sunlight, droplets of soil beading in the air about her. Resubmerging, she would strike out for the cool solitude of the clay and sandstone, far, far beneath her...

Someone walked across the surface of the black water, wooden sandals scuffing audibly against its suddenly hardened substance, crunching through leaves that were quite dry. Unable to sustain itself before such contradictions, the illusion melted and was immediately beyond recall.

One side of Som-Som's face clouded in annoyance at this intrusion upon her reverie, half her brow clenching into a petulant frown while the other half remained uncreased and indifferent. Her single visible eye, one from a pair of gems made more exquisite by the loss of its twin, glared down at the visitor passing beneath her. Unnoticed upon her balcony, she studied the interloper, struck suddenly by some quirk of gait or posture that seemed familiar. Her left eye squinted slightly as she strained for a better view, deforming the symmetry of her bisected face into a mirthless wink.

The figure was slender and of medium height, swathed in gorgeous bandages of red silk from crown to ankle so that only the face, hands, and feet were left unwrapped. The delicate line of the shoulder and arm seemed unmistakably female, but there remained something masculine about the manner in which the torso joined with the narrow, angular hips. Walking unhurriedly across the courtyard, it paused before the pale yellow door that lay at the rightmost extremity of the House Without Clocks. There the figure hesitated, turning to survey the courtyard and giving Som-Som her first clear glimpse of a painted face at once strikingly alien and instantly recognizable.

The visitor's name was Rawra Chin, and She was a man.

During the years of her service within that drifting environment, her perceptions of the world limited both by her condition and by the virtual confinement that was its effective result, Som-Som had nonetheless contrived to reach a plateau of understanding, an internal vantage point overlooking the vast sphere of human activity from which the Broken Mask had excluded her. This perspective afforded her certain insights that were at once acute and peculiar.

She understood, for example, that quite apart from being a limitless ocean of fortune, the world was also a churning maelstrom of sex. Establishments such as the House Without Clocks were islands within that current, where people were washed ashore by the tides of need and loneliness. Some would remain there forever, lodged upon the high-tide line. Most would be sucked away when the ebb of the waters came. Of these fragments reclaimed by the ocean, few would ever again reach land, and if they did it would not be in those latitudes.

Rawra Chin, it seemed, was an exception.

Som-Som remembered Her as a wide-boned and awkward boy of fourteen whose employment at the House Without Clocks had commenced when Som-Som was already in the fifth year of her service. Despite the flatness and breadth of Her face and the clumsiness of Her deportment, Rawra Chin had even than possessed some rare and indefinable essence of personality, animating the uneasy frame of the adolescent boy and lending Her a beauty that was disturbing in its effect.

Mistress Ouish, long skilled in detecting that pearl of the remarkable that is concealed within the oyster of the ordinary, had noticed Rawra Chin's distinct yet elusive charm when she decided to employ the youth. So, too, did the clientele of the House Without Clocks, with numerous merchants, fishermen and soldiers proclaiming Her their especial favorite, asking after Her whenever they should chance to visit that establishment.

The common bond shared by all those who admired this charisma within Rawra Chin was that none of them could precisely identify it. It remained a mystery, concealed somewhere within the oddly disparate components of Her broad and starkly decorated face, hovering at some imaginary point of focus between Her hasty pencil-line of a mouth and Her widely-spaced eyes, overwhelmingly tangible, eternally ungraspable.

Som-Som, one of two people within the House who came to know Rawra Chin closely, had always been inclined to the belief that Her charms originated in the emotional depths of the nervous and hesitant lad Herself, rather than in some fluke of physique or physiognomy.

There was a restless melancholy that seemed to inform everything from the boy's stance to the way She brushed Her hair, long and soft, so golden it was almost white. There was also the occasional icicle glitter of fear in those eyes that had too great a distance between them for prettiness but just enough for beauty. These disparate threads of personality were woven into a design that gave the overwhelming impression of vulnerability. As to the precise nature of that vulnerability, Som-Som had no more idea than the most brief and casual of Rawra's adoring customers.

Often, She had come to sit and drink tea with Som-Som upon her balcony to pass the time between engagements, a diversion popular with many of the inhabitants of the House Without Clocks. Due to the singularity of Som-Som's impairment, they could reveal their longings or resentments without fear. Rawra Chin had visited her often during the long, dull mornings, seeming to delight in the thin floral infusions and the opportunity for one-sided conversation.

It seemed to Som-Som that she had contributed little to these often intimate discussions, having no confidences that she was able to share. Since the side of her brain that governed speech had known nothing but darkness and silence for several years, the best that it could offer conversationally was a string of inappropriate and disconnected fragments, half-remembered impressions and anecdotes relating to the world that Som-Som had known before the Silencing.

Confusing matters further, Som-Som's verbal half could not hear and was forced to make interjections without knowing whether the other person had finished speaking. Thus, while Rawra Chin would be engaged in a vivid description of what She hoped to do once Her employment at the House Without Clocks was ended, Som-Som would startle Her by saying, "I remember that my mother was an unlikable woman who rushed everywhere to get her life over with the sooner," or something equally obscure, followed by a long silence during which she would stare politely at Rawra Chin and sip her floral infusion through the left corner of her mouth.

Though at first disoriented by these random pronunciations, Rawra Chin grew accustomed to them, waiting until Som-Som had finished her non sequitur before resuming. The continuing presence of these bizarre ejaculations did not seem to lessen Rawra Chin's enjoyment of their conversational interludes. Som-Som supposed that her real contribution to these talks had been her simple presence.

Her function was that of a receptacle for the aspirations and anxieties of others, although this fact never became oppressive. She enjoyed the exclusiveness of these glimpses into the way that ordinary life was conducted. The fact that people would relate to her things that went unvoiced even to their lovers gave Som-Som a perspective upon human nature more true and comprehensive than that enjoyed by many sages and philosophers.

This gave her a measure of personal power, and she

took pride in her ability to unravel the many and varied personas that presented themselves to her, laying bare the essential characteristics that were concealed beneath their facades of affectation and self-deception. Rawra Chin had been Som-Som's only failure. Like everyone else, she had been unable to give a name to that rare and precious element upon which the bewilderingly attractive adolescent boy had founded Her identity.

On the other hand, Som-Som had been able to construct a relatively complete picture of Rawra Chin's aversions and ambitions, however superficial these appeared without an understanding of Her more fundamental motivations.

Som-Som knew, for example, that Rawra Chin did not intend to make a lifetime's vocation of prostitution. While she had heard similar avowals from most of the occupants of the House Without Clocks, Som-Som sensed a determination in Rawra Chin that was iron-hard, setting Her appraisal of the future apart from the rather sad and much-thumbed fantasies of Her fellows.

Rawra Chin, She often assured Som-Som, would one day be a great performer who would travel the globe, transporting Her art to the masses by way of a celebrated company of dramaticians such as the Torn Stocking Troupe, or Dimuk Paparian's Mnemonic Players. The less aesthetically demanding acts of pantomime that She was called upon to perform each day behind the pale yellow door of the House Without

Clocks were merely a clumsy rehearsal for the innumerable thespian triumphs waiting somewhere in Her future.

The pale yellow door gave access to that part of the house that was given over to romantic pursuits of a more theatrical nature, its four floors each housing a single specialist in the erotic arts, linked by a polished wooden staircase that zigzagged up outside the house from courtyard level toward the gray slate incline of the roof.

In the topmost chamber lived Mopetel, the corpse-mime. Beneath her lived Loba Pak, whose flesh had a freakish consistency that enabled her to adjust her features into the semblance of almost any woman between the ages of fourteen and seventy. Rawra Chin lived upon the second floor, acting out mundane and unimaginative roles for Her eager male clientele but compensating for this with Her charisma. On the first floor, immediately beyond the pale yellow door, there lived a brilliant and savagely passionate male actor named Foral Yatt whose talent had been subverted into a plaything by the many female customers who enjoyed his company, and with whom Rawra Chin had become amorously entangled.

Foral Yatt was the subject of a great number of those balcony conversations, conducted through the motionless fog of warm vapor that hung above their tea bowls, with Rawra Chin talking animatedly upon one side while Som-Som sat listening upon the other, breaking her silence intermittently to remark that she remembered the color of a quilt her grandmother had made for her when she was an infant, or that a brother whose name she could no longer call to mind had once knocked over the pot-boil and badly scalded his legs.

The heart of Rawra Chin's anguish concerning Foral Yatt seemed to lie in Her knowledge that if She were to achieve Her ambition, She must leave the intense and darkly attractive young actor while She progressed to greater things. She confessed to Som-Som that though in private She and Foral Yatt would make their plans as if they would quit the House Without Clocks together, pursuing parallel careers in the outside world, Rawra Chin knew that this was a fiction.

Despite the fact that Foral Yatt's raw talent dwarfed Her own to insignificance, he possessed neither the indefinable appeal of Rawra Chin or the remoreseless drive that would propel him through the pale yellow door and into the pitch and swell of that better life that lay beyond. Adding masochistically to Her anguish, the wide-faced boy also felt troubled by the fact that She was using Her nearness to Foral Yatt to study the finer points of his superior craft, storing each nuance of characterization, each breathtakingly understated gesture, until that point in Her career-to-come when She might use them.

Having purged Herself for the moment of Her moral burden, Rawra Chin would sit and stare miserably at Som-Som, waiting for some acknowledgment of Her dilemma. Long moments would pass, measured in whatever units were appropriate within the House Without Clocks, until finally Som-Som would smile and say, "It was raining on the afternoon that I almost choked on a pebble," or "Her name was either Mur or Mar, and I think that she was my sister," after which Rawra Chin would finish Her tea and leave, feeling obscurely contented.

Despite Her tormented writhings, Rawra Chin had eventually summoned sufficient strength of character or sufficient callousness to inform Foral Yatt that She would be leaving him, having been offered a place in a small but critically acclaimed touring company by a customer who transpired to be the merchant without whose continuing financial support the company could not survive.

Som-Som could still remember the ugly playlet that the two estranged lovers had performed in the courtyard of the House on the morning that Rawra Chin was to leave. While the other inhabitants watched with boredom or amusement from their balconies, the players paced across the flat black stage, seemingly oblivious to the audience that watched from above as their angry accusals and sullen denials rang from the curving courtyard walls.

Foral Yatt pathetically followed Rawra Chin around the courtyard, almost staggering beneath the weight of the dreadful, unexpected betrayal. He was a tall, lean man with beautiful arms, his eyes dark and deep set, brimming with tears as he trailed behind Rawra Chin, an unwanted satellite still trapped within Her orbit by the irresistible gravity of Her mystique. The fact that he kept his skull shaven to a close stubble to facilitate the numerous changes of wig required by his customers only added to his air of desolation.

Rawra Chin remained a measured number of paces in front of him, occasionally directing some pained but dignified comment over Her shoulder while he ranted, incoherent with hurt, raging and confused. Som-Som suspected that She was in some oblique way enjoying this abuse from Her former lover, that She accepted his tirade as an inverted tribute to Her mesmeric influence over him.

Eventually, when desperation had driven Foral Yatt beyond all considerations of dignity, he threatened to kill himself. Pulling something from the small pouch that he wore at his belt, the distraught young actor held it aloft so that it glittered in the morning sunlight.

It was a miniature human skull, fashioned from green glass and holding no more than a mouthful of the clear, licorice-scented liquid that it had been designed to contain. No more than a mouthful was required. These suicidal trinkets could be purchased quite openly, and it was impossible to determine how many of Liavek's more pessimistically inclined citizens carried one of the death's-heads in anticipation of that day when life was no longer endurable.

His voice ragged with emotion, Foral Yatt swore that he would not be deserted in so casual a manner. He promised to end his life if Rawra Chin did not pick up Her baggage and carry it back through the pale yellow door to their chambers.

They stared at each other, and Som-Som had thought that she perceived a flicker of uncertainty dance across the widely-spaced eyes of the young boy as they moved from Foral Yatt's face to the skull-shaped bottle in his hand. The instant seemed to inflate into a massive balloon of silence, punctured by the sudden rattle of hooves and wheels from beyond the courtyard's arched entrance, signaling the arrival of the carriage that was to take Rawra Chin to join Her theater troupe. She darted one last glance at Foral Yatt and then, picking up Her baggage, turned and walked out through the archway.

Foral Yatt stood transfixed at the center of the huge black disc, still with one flawless arm raised, clutching its cold green fistful of oblivion. He stared blankly at the archway as if expecting her to reappear and tell him it was all some ill-considered hoax. From beyond the encircling walls there came the jingle of reins followed by a slow clattering and the creaking of wood and leather as the carriage moved away down the winding streets of the City of Luck. After a pause during which it seemed that he would never move again, the actor slowly and falteringly lowered his arm.

Three floors above him, realizing the abandoned lover wouldn't kill himself, one of the denizens of the House Without Clocks pursed her shiny black lips discontentedly and made a clucking sound before retiring to her quarters. Hearing the sound, Foral Yatt tilted back his gray-stubbled skull and stared up at the watchers in surprise, as if previously unaware of their scrutiny. His eyes were full of miserable incomprehension, and it was a relief to Som-Som when he lowered them to the black tiles at his feet before walking slowly across the courtyard toward the pale yellow door, the glass skull now quite forgotten in his hand.

Scarcely a handful of months elapsed before news began to work its way back to the House Without Clocks of Rawra Chin's dizzying success. It seemed that Her elusive charisma was able to captivate audiences as easily as it had once enthralled Her individual customers. Her performance as the tragic and infertile Queen Gorda in Mossoc's *The Crib* was already the talk of Liavek's intelligentsia, and rumor had it that a special performance for His Scarlet Eminence was being considered.

Such talk was generally kept from the inconsolable

Foral Yatt, but within the year Rawra Chin's fame had spread to the point where the embittered young actor was as aware of it as anyone. He seemed to take the news of Her stellar ascent with less resentment than might have been anticipated, once the initial despair of separation had lifted from him. Indeed, save for a coldness that would creep into his eyes at the mention of Her name, Foral Yatt made much of his indifference to his former lover's fortunes. He never spoke of Her, and those less insightful than Som-Som might have supposed that he had forgotten Her altogether.

Now, five years later, She had returned.

In the courtyard beneath Som-Som's balcony, Rawra Chin turned to face the pale yellow door, a resigned slump in Her shoulders. She lifted one hand to knock, and there was a sudden dazzling scintillation that seemed to play about Her fingers. It took Som-Som a moment to realize that the young man had chips of some reflective substance pasted to Her nails. The afternoon was hushed, as if holding its breath while it listened, and the sound of Rawra Chin's white knuckles upon the pale yellow wood was disproportionately loud.

Seated high above on her balcony, Som-Som found that she wanted desperately to call out, to warn Rawra Chin that it was a mistake to return to this place, that She should leave immediately. Silence, massive and absolute, surrounded her and would not permit her to make the smallest sound. She was embedded in silence, a tiny bubble of consciousness within a infinity of solid rock, mute and gray and endless. She struggled against it, willing her tongue to shape the vital words of warning, knowing as she did so that it was hopeless.

Below, someone unlocked the pale yellow door from inside and it creaked once, musically, as it opened. It was too late.

Som-Som's balcony was situated upon the third floor, the adjacent living area being one of four contained behind the violet door at the extreme left of the House Without Clocks' concave front. Thus, as she sat upon her balcony and gazed down at Rawra Chin she could not see who had opened the door. She supposed that it was Foral Yatt.

There was a surprising low exchange of words, following which the crimson-wrapped figure of the celebrated performer stepped inside the house and beyond Som-Som's vision. The pale yellow door closed with a sound like something sucking its teeth.

After that, there was only silence. Som-Som remained seated upon her balcony staring down at the pale yellow door with mute anguish in her one visible eye while the sky gradually darkened behind her. Finally, when the moment of her urgent need for a voice was long past, she spoke.

"I ran as fast as I could, but when I reached my mother's house the bird was already dead."

∎

Since the closing of the yellow door, no word had been spoken in the rooms that lay immediately behind it. Foral Yatt sat in a hard wooden chair beside the open fire, amber light flickering across one side of his lean face. Rawra Chin stood by the window, Her vivid crimson darkening to a dull, scablike burgundy against the failing light outside. Uncertain of how best to gauge the distance that had arisen between them, She watched the play of firelight upon the velvet of his shaven skull until the absence of conversation was more than she could endure.

"I brought you a gift." Foral Yatt slowly turned his head toward Her, away from the fire, so that the shadow slid across his face, and his expression was no longer visible. Rawra Chin immersed one chalk-white hand in the black fur of the bag She carried, from whence it emerged holding a small copper ball between the mirror-tipped fingers. She held it out to him and, after a moment, he took it.

"What is it?"

She had forgotten how captivating his voice was, dry and deep and hungry, quite unlike Her own. Calm and evenly modulated, there remained a sense of something watchful and carnivorous lurking just beyond it, pacing quietly behind the accents and

Rawra Chin licked her lips.

"It's a toy...a toy of the intellect. I'm told that it's very relaxing. Many of the busiest merchants that I know find that it calms them immeasurably after the bustle of commerce."

Foral Yatt turned the smooth copper sphere between his fingers so that it gleamed red in the glow of the fire.

"What's so special about it?"

Rawra Chin took a step away from the window, Her first tentative movement toward him since entering the House, and then paused. She let Her black fur bag drop with a soft thud, like the corpse of an enormous spider, onto the empty seat of the room's other chair. A certain establishing of territory accompanied the gesture, and Rawra Chin hoped She had not overstepped in Her eagerness. Foral Yatt's face was still in shadow, but he did not seem to react adversely to the wedge-end represented by the bag dozing before the hearth. Encouraged by this lack of obvious rebuke, Rawra Chin smiled, albeit nervously, as She replied to him.

"There might be a lizard asleep inside the ball, or there might not. That's the puzzle."

His silence seemed to invite elaboration.

"The story goes that there exists a lizard capable of hibernating for years or even centuries without food or air or moisture, slowing its vital processes so that a dozen winters might pass between each beat of its heart. I am told that it is a very small creature, no bigger than the top joint of my thumb when it is curled up.

"The people who make these ornaments allegedly place one of the sleeping reptiles inside each ball before sealing it. If you look closely, you can see that there's a seam around the middle."

Foral Yatt declined to do so, remaining seated, his back toward the fire, holding the ball in his right hand and turning it so that molten highlights rolled across its surface. Though an impenetrable shadow still concealed his expression, Rawra Chin sensed that the quality of his silence had changed. She felt whatever slight advantage She had gained begin to slip away. Why wouldn't he speak? Unable to keep the edge of unease from Her voice, She resumed Her monologue.

"You can't open it, and, and you have to think about whether there really is a lizard inside it or not. It's to do with how we perceive the world around us, and when you think about it you start to see that it doesn't matter if there's a lizard inside there or not, and then you can think about what's real and what isn't real, and..."

Her voice trailed off, as if suddenly aware of its own incoherence.

"...and it's said to be very relaxing," She concluded lamely, after a flat, dismal pause.

"Why did you come back?"

"I don't know."

"You don't know."

It was as if Her words had hit a mirror, rebounding back at Her full of new meanings and implications, warped out of true by some fluke of the glass. Rawra Chin's fragile composure began to crumble before that flat, disinterested voice.

"I...I don't mean that I don't know. I just mean..."

She look down at Her pale, well-kept hands to find that She was wringing them together. They looked like crabs mating after having been kept in the dark for too long

"I mean that there was no real reason for me to come back here. My work, my career, it's all too perfect. I have a lot of money. I have friends. I've just completed my role as Bromar's eldest daughter in *The Lucksmith* and everybody will talk about me for months. For a while, I do not have to work. I can do whatever I want.

"I didn't have to come back here."

Foral Yatt remained silent, the firelight behind his shaven head edging his skull with a trim of blurred phosphorescence as it shone through the stubble. The copper ball turned between his fingers, a miniature planet rolling from day into night.

"It's just that...this place, this house, it has something. There's something inside this house, and it's something true. It isn't a good thing. It's just a true thing, and I don't know what the name of it is, and I don't even like it, but I know that it's true and I know that it's here and I felt, I don't know, I felt that I had to come back and look at it. It's like..."

Rawra Chin's hands seemed to pluck and squeeze the air before Her, as if the words She required were concealed beneath its skin, and that by probing She could guess at their shape. Separated now, the blanched crustacean lovers lay upon their backs, feebly waving their legs as they expired upon some unseen shoreline.

"It's like an accident I saw...a farmer, crushed beneath his cart. He was alive, but his ribs were broken and sticking through his side. I didn't know what they were at first, because it was all such a mess. There were a lot of people gathered 'round, but nobody could move the cart without hurting him even more than he was hurt already.

"It was summer, and there were a lot of flies. I remember him screaming and shouting for somebody to beat the flies away, and an old woman went out and did that for him, but until then nobody had moved, not until he screamed at them. It was horrible. I walked by as fast as I could because he was suffering and there was nothing anybody could do, except for the old woman who was beating the flies away with her apron.

"But I went back.

"I stopped just a little way down the road, and I

went back. I couldn't help it. I was just that it was so real and so painful, that man, lying there under that terrible weight and screaming for his wife, his children, it was so real that it just cut through everything else in the world, all the things that my luck and my money have built up around me, and I knew that it meant something, and I went back there and I watched him drown on his own blood while the old woman told him not to worry, that his wife and children would be there soon.

"And that's why I came back to the House Without Clocks."

There was a long hyphen of silence. A copper world rotated between the fingers of a faceless and unanswering god.

"And I still love you."

Someone rapped twice upon the pale yellow door.

For a moment there was no movement within the room save for the illusion of motion engendered by the firelight. Then Foral Yatt rose from the hard wooden chair, still with the fire at his back and his face in eclipse. Crossing the room, ducking beneath the blackened beams that supported the low ceiling, he passed close enough for Her to raise Her hand and brush his arm, so that it would be thought an accident of passing. But She didn't.

Foral Yatt opened the door.

The figure on the other side of the threshold was

perhaps forty years of age, a large and strong-boned woman with raw cheeks who wore a single garment like a tent of smoky gray fur. It covered the top of her head with a hole cut away to reveal the face, and then its striking, minimal lines dropped away to the floor. There was no opening in the fur through which she might extend her hands, which suggested to Rawra Chin that the woman must have servants to do everything for her, the feeding to her of meals not excluded. Even in the world that Rawra Chin had known over the previous five years, such arrogantly flaunted wealth was impressive.

As the inopportune visitor tilted back her head to speak, the flickering yellow light caught her face, and Rawra Chin noticed that the woman had an amber blemish, unpleasantly furry-looking, that almost entirely covered her left cheek. The woman had obviously attempted to conceal it beneath a thick coat of white powder with little success. The discoloration remained visible through the makeup as if it were a paper-thin flatfish that swam through her subcutaneous tissue, its dark shape discernible just below the clouded surface of her face.

When she spoke, her voice was distressingly loud, her tone strident and somehow abusive.

"Foral Yatt. Dear Foral Yatt, how long? How long has it been since I saw you last?"

Foral Yatt's reply was professionally polite, cooly

inoffensive, and yet delivered at such volume that Rawra Chin winced involuntarily, even though She stood several paces behind him. It came to Her suddenly that the fur-draped woman must suffer from some defect of hearing.

"It has been two days since you were here, Donna Blerot. I have missed you."

A wave of hotness washed over Rawra Chin, cooling almost instantly to a leaden ingot in Her stomach. Foral Yatt had a customer, and She must leave him to his labors. Her disappointment was so big She could not admit that it was Hers. She resolved to leave immediately, hoping to keep it one step behind Her until She could reach Her own rooms in a lodging house on the far side of the City of Luck. Once She was safely behind closed door she would let it have its way with Her, and then there would be tears. She was reaching for Her bag, sleeping there in its chair, when Foral Yatt spoke again.

"However, it is not convenient that I should see you tonight. A member of my family has come to visit"—here he gestured vaguely over his shoulder toward the stunned Rawra Chin—"and I regret that you and I must let our yearnings simmer untended for one more day. Please be patient, Donna Blerot. When finally we meet together, you know that our union will be the sweeter for this postponement."

Donna Blerot turned her head and gazed past Foral

Yatt at the slim, crimson-swathed figure that stood in the flamelit room, almost like a flame Herself within the gaudy wrappings. The dame's eyes were frozen and merciless, boring into Rawra Chin for long instants before she turned them once more toward Foral Yatt, her expression softening.

"This is too bad, Foral Yatt. Simply too bad. But I shall forgive you. How could I ever do otherwise?"

She smiled, her teeth yellow and her lips too wide.

"Until tomorrow, then?"

"Until tomorrow, dearest Donna Blerot."

The woman turned from the door and Rawra Chin heard the slow, derisive clapping of her wooden sandals as she walked back across the black courtyard. Foral Yatt closed the door, sliding the bolt across. The sound of the bolt's passage, metal against metal, was electrifying in its implications, and Rawra Chin shuddered in resonance. The actor turned away from the closed portal and stared at Her, his face brazen in the fire glow.

His face seemed less chiseled and gaunt than She had remembered it. His eyes, conversely, were so riveting and intense that She knew Her recollection had not done them justice. Across a chamber so filled with swaying clots of darkness that it seemed like a ballroom for shadows, the two young men stared at each other. Neither spoke.

He walked toward Her, pausing only to set the

small copper globe upon the polished white wood of his tabletop before continuing. His pace was so deliberate that Rawra Chin felt sure he must be aware of the tension that this deliciously prolonged approach kindled within Her. Unable to meet his gaze, She lowered Her lashes so that the quivering light of the room became streaks of incoherent brilliance. Her breathing grew shallow, and she trembled.

The warm, dry smell of his skin enveloped Her. She knew that he was standing just before Her, no more than a forearm's length away. Then he touched Her face. The shock of physical contact almost caused her to jerk Her head back, but She controlled the impulse. Her heart rang like an anvil as his fingernail traced the line of Her jaw.

The ingenious arrangement of bandages that was Rawra Chin's costume had a single fastening, concealed behind a triangular black gem in a filigree surround that She wore upon the right side of Her throat. The pin pricked Her neck as Foral Yatt withdrew it from the blood-red windings, but even this seemed almost unbearably pleasant to Her in that aching, oversensitized state. She lifted Her gaze and his eyes swallowed Her whole. With his hands moving in languid, confident circles, he began to unwind the long band of brightly dyed gauze, starting from Her head and spiraling downward.

Free of the confining wrap, Her thick hair tumbled

down upon Her white shoulders. She gasped and shook Her head from side to side, but it was not an indication of denial. A wave of thrilling coolness crept down Her body as progressively more of Her skin was exposed to the drafts of the room. It moved across Her belly and down to the angular and jutting hips, over the shaven pudenda and past the jumping, half-erect penis. It continued down Her thighs and on toward the rush carpeting, where the unraveled wrappings gathered in a widening red puddle about Her feet, as if Her naked flesh bled from a dozen imperceptible wounds.

He nodded his head to Her once, still without a sound, and She knelt upon the floor at his feet, Her knees pressed against the tangle of fallen bandages so that they would leave a faint lattice of impressions upon Her skin. Closing Her eyes, She allowed Her head to sink forward until it came to rest against the seat of the chair in which She had placed Her bag an eternity before. Its luscious dark fur and the hard wood were equally cool against Her burning cheek.

Behind Her, a single brief chime, Foral Yatt's buckle dropped unceremoniously to the rush matting. Upon an impulse, She allowed Her eyes to open, their gaze drifting across the chamber, drinking in the moment in all its infinitesimal detail. On the other side of the room, the copper ball rested upon the tabletop where Foral Yatt had placed it. It was like the freshly gouged eye of a brazen speaking-head, such as certain personages in Wizard's Row were reputed to possess.

It stared back at Rawra Chin, glittering suggestively, and all that came to pass behind the pale yellow door was reflected impartially, in perfect miniature, upon the convex surface of that lifeless and unblinking orb.

Later, lying flat upon Her stomach with their mingled sweat drying in the hollow of Her back, Rawra Chin allowed Her awareness to float tethered upon the margins of wakefulness while Foral Yatt squatted naked by the fire, adding fresh coals to sustain a fading redness that had burned low during the preceding hour. The air was heavy with the intoxicating bouquet of semen, and each of Her muscles slumped in blissful exhaustion.

Still, something nagged at Her, even in the sublime depths of her sated torpor. There was yet something unresolved between the two of them, no matter how eloquent their lovemaking may have seemed. It was barely a real thing at all, more a disquieting absence than an intrusive presence, and She might have ignored it. This, however, proved more than She could bear. It was a cavity within Her that must be filled before She could be complete. Though reluctant to send ripples through the calm afterglow of their congress, eventually She found Her voice.

"Do you still love me?" This was followed, after a hesitant beat, by, "Despite what I did to you?"

She turned Her head so that the right side of Her

face rested against the interwoven rushes. He crouched before the fire with his back toward Her as he carefully arranged cold black nuggets atop the bright embers. His skin glistened, a yellow smear of watercolor highlight running down the side toward the fire. She followed the line of his vertebrae with Her eyes to the plumbline-straight crease that bisected the hard buttocks, adoring him. He did not turn to Her as he replied.

"Is there a lizard asleep within the ball?"

Taking another piece of coal in a hand already blackened by dust, Foral Yatt placed a capstone atop the dark pyramid in the scaled-down hell of the fireplace. Nothing more was said behind the pale yellow door that night.

Upon the following morning, Rawra Chin visited Som-Som and took tea with her, as if the five-year hiatus in their ritual had never existed. She recounted a string of anecdotes from Her career, than paused to sip Her infusion while Som-Som informed Her that her mother had once closed a door, and that it had once been dark, and that once she had been unable to stop coughing. Rawra Chin's smooth re-entry into the bizarre rhythms of their conversation did much to eradicate any distance between the two that might have flourished in their half decade of separation. Even so, it was not until the interlude approached its conclusion that the performer felt comfortable enough to broach the subject of Her resumed relationship with Foral Yatt.

"I won't be staying here forever, of course. In another month or so I must begin to consider my next role, and it would be impossible to do that here. But this time, when I leave, I believe I shall take him with me. I'm rich enough to keep him until he finds work of his own, and it seems ridiculous that someone with his talent should be wasting it upon..."

Her hands performed a curious movement that was part theatrical gesture and part genuine involuntary revulsion. It was as if they were retching with violent spasms that shuddered out from the slender throat of the wrist and on toward Her fingertips, where ten mirrors shivered in the cold morning sunlight.

"...upon ugly, sick old women like that terrible Donna Blerot! He deserves so much better. I could look after him, I could find work for him, and then perhaps neither of us would need to come back to this place ever again, not even just to look at it. Don't you think that would be a good idea?"

Som-Som sipped her floral infusion through the corner of her mouth and said nothing.

"I think we can do it. I think that we can love each other and be together without anything going wrong between us. It was only my ambition that pushed us apart before, and I've fulfilled that now. Things can be just as they were, only somewhere else, in a better place than this."

Rawra Chin looked so thoughtful, sucking the dazzling tip of Her right index finger so that it made a small and liquid popping sound when she pulled it from between Her lips. She did this twice. Behind Her, birds wheeled above the diverse skyline of Liavek. When She spoke again, Her voice had assumed a puzzled tone.

"Of course, he has changed. I suppose we've both changed. He's very quiet now, and very...very commanding. Yes, that's it exactly. Very commanding. It's wonderful, I'm not complaining at all. After all, those are his chambers and he's being kind enough to let me stay there for the next couple of months so that I don't need to keep up my rooms at the lodging house. I don't mind doing whatever he wants. I think, you know, I think it's good for me in a way, good for how I am as a person. Since my career broke out of the egg, nobody had told me what to do. I think that's spoiled me. It doesn't feel right, somehow. Not when people just defer to me all the time. I think I need someone to—"

"A sticky head looked out from between the cow's legs, and I screamed."

Som-Som's interjection was so startling that even Rawra Chin, accustomed to such utterances, was momentarily unnerved. Blinking, She waited to see if the half masked woman intended to make any further comment before continuing.

"I'm having my clothes sent over from the lodging house. I have so many beautiful things it hardly seems fair. Foral Yatt says that he will store my wardrobe, but he does not want me to wear the more exotic creations while I am with him. He prefers plainer things."

Rawra Chin glanced down at the clothing She was dressed in. She wore a simple blouse of gray cotton and a skirt of similar material. Her white-gold hair swung about Her narrow shoulders and sparked life from the dusk-colored fabric with its contrast. It lay against Her blouse like wan torchlight reflected on wet, gray cobbles. Evidently satisfied with the novel restraint and subtlety of her costume, She raised Her lashes and smiled across the tea bowls at Som-Som.

"But enough of my affairs and vanities. Which side of luck have you yourself walked these five years gone?"

The divided face stared back at Her with its one live eye. No one spoke. Over the City of Luck, great scavenger birds dipped and shrieked, so that it sounded as if babies had been torn up from the earth and dragged wailing into the oppressive dome of the sky.

On the fifth day after Her arrival, Rawra Chin appeared upon Som-Som's balcony wearing breeches of leather with a stout length of rope looped about the waist as a belt. She did not refer to this reversal of Her sartorial tendencies, but after that Som-Som never again saw Her in a skirt and supposed that this was due to Foral Yatt's austere influence. The performer seemed also to forgo the application of face paint and the wearing of all jewelry save for a simple band of unadorned iron, which She wore upon the smallest finger of Her left hand. The ten slivers of mirror were long since vanished.

Two weeks after Her return, Foral Yatt persuaded Rawra Chin to shave off Her hair.

Sitting with Som-Som the following morning, She would break off from Her trail of conversation every few seconds and run one incredulous palm back from Her temple and across the stubble. Her talk had a forced gaiety, and there was something nervous and darting within Her eyes. Som-Som realized with some surprise that Rawra Chin no longer seemed attractive. It was as if Her charisma had leaked out of Her, or been sheared away as ruthlessly as the spun sunlight of Her hair.

"I think, I think I look better like this, don't you?"

Som-Som said nothing.

"I mean to say that it, well, it makes such a change. And I think it will do my hair a service, after it grows back. The colorings I use had made it so brittle, a new head of hair will be such a relief. And of course, Foral Yatt likes it this way."

The casual delivery of this last phrase was belied by an evasive glance and an air of restless self-consciousness.

"I mean, I understand how it must look, how it must look to people who don't know him, but..."

One hand rasped lightly across Her skull in a single, backward motion.

"...but the way that I dress is important to him, the way I look, it's so important to him, the way that I look when we make love."

Som-Som cleared her throat and told the performer the name of the street where she had lived before the night when her mother had led her out by the hand, through the noise and toward the Silence. Rawra Chin continued Her monologue without acknowledging the interjection, Her eyes hollow and sleepless with their gaze still fixed on the grubby tiles.

"He's changed, you see. He wants different things now. And, and I don't mind. I love him. I don't mind what he wants me to do. I even like it, sometimes I like it for myself and not just for him. But the fact, the fact that I like it, that's something that frightens me. Not frightens me, really, but it's as if everything is changing and moving under my feet, and as if I'm changing too, and I feel as if I should be frightened, but I'm not. It's so easy, just slipping into it. It's so easy just to let it happen, and I don't mind. I love him and I don't mind."

From the dilated pupil of the courtyard, someone called Rawra Chin's name. Som-Som turned her gaze to the flagstones below, puzzling for a moment over the stranger who stood there before she was able to reconcile the familiar face with the unplaceable gait and manner, finally resolving these disparate impressions into Foral Yatt.

Rawra Chin had spoken the truth. Foral Yatt had changed.

Standing beneath them, looking up with one hand raised to shield his eyes from the sun, the bar of shadow cast across his features did not conceal the change that had come over them. The actor seemed less lean. Som-Som supposed that this was in part due to Rawra Chin's wealth supplementing his income and his diet.

His clothing, too, was noticeably different from the somber and functional raiment that he had appeared to favor. Foral Yatt wore a long tunic, its blue so deep and vibrant that it bordered upon iridescence. A wide orange sash was wound twice about his waist, and the billowing pants that he wore beneath were orange also, a fragile, mottled orange almost white in places. His feet were naked and exquisite, much smaller then Som-Som would have expected them to be. Something glittered, a sparkling fog about the toes.

"Rawra Chin? Our meal is almost prepared."

His voice had altered, too: lighter, a patina of melody imposed upon its assured tones. And there was something else, something which above all was responsible for the striking change in his aspect, something so obvious that it eluded her completely.

Rawra Chin murmured an apology as She made ready to leave, not bothering to tie up any loose ends remaining from Her conversation with Som-Som. As was Her custom, She reached out and squeezed Som-Som's wrist to let the half of her brain that was cut off from sight or sound know that her visitor was leaving. In response, the half-masked woman lifted her gaze until it met Rawra Chin's. When she spoke, her voice was filled with a sadness that seemed to have no bearing upon the content of her speech.

"I do not think that the good was so good, back then."

Rawra Chin's lips twitched once, a helpless little facial shrug, and then She turned and ran down the narrow wooden stairs that led to the courtyard below, where Foral Yatt awaited Her.

She joined him there and they exchanged a snatch of dialogue that was too low for Som-Som to hear before making their way toward the pale yellow door. Som-Som craned her neck to watch them go. Just before they passed from her sight, she identified the single glaring quirk that had so transformed the young actor.

Running along his brow in an uneven snow-line, curling around the topmost rim of his ears, Foral Yatt's hair was starting to grow out.

On the fifteenth night after Her arrival at the House

Without Clocks, something occurred behind the pale yellow door that gave Rawra Chin Her first glimpse into the darkness that had been waiting for Her for five long years. She went indoors to share Her evening repast with Foral Yatt just as the sun was butchering the western horizon, and before morning She had seen the abyss. She was not to comprehend the immensity of the hungry void beneath Her for some three days further, but that first shattering look was the beginning. It was as if She dropped a pebble into the chasm that awaited Her and listened for the splash. When three days later the splash had still not come, She knew that the blackness was bottomless, and that there was no hope.

On the earlier evening, however, when She walked through the pale yellow door with the sunset at Her back and the rich aroma of the pot-boil hanging before Her, this shadow was yet to fall. It seemed to Her that all her anxieties were containable.

They ate their meal quickly, the two of them facing each other across the blanched wood of the table, and then Rawra Chin cleared away what debris there was while Foral Yatt retired to his bedchamber to prepare for the business of the evening ahead. Rawra Chin, scraping an obstinate scab of dried legume from the lip of his bowl, wondered idly what She would find to amuse Herself tonight during the hours when Her presence behind the pale yellow door was not required. On previous nights she had walked down to the harbor.

Watching the moon's reflection in the iron-green water, She had tried to wring some cooling trickle of romance from Her situation.

With an abbreviated cry of pain and surprise She looked down to discover that She had split Her nail upon the nub of dried and hardened food. Her nails were a ruin, She thought, all of them bitten and uneven, many of them split or with raw pink about the quick. She wondered how long it would take for them to regain their former elegance, and as She did so She ran Her other hand back over Her razed scalp without being aware of the gesture.

Foral Yatt called to Her from the bedchamber and she went to see what he wanted, wiping Her hands upon the coarse gray fabric of Her shirt as She trudged across the rush matting.

Stepping through the door of the chamber, she was puzzled to discover that Foral Yatt had retired to bed, rather than preparing for the evening's duties. He lay upon the rough cotton of the sheets with his eyes half-closed and his hands resting limp upon the patches of dyed sackcloth that formed the counterpane.

"I cannot work this evening. I am ill."

Rawra Chin's brow knotted into a frown. He did not look discomforted nor was his voice unsteady or less masterful, and yet he said that he was sick. It was as if he meant Her to understand that this was a lie but to respond as if it were irrefutable truth.

Searching within Herself She discovered, with only the briefest pang of surprise or disappointment, that She did not mind. She accommodated the fiction, because that was the easiest thing to do.

"But what of Mistress Ouish? There have been other nights lately when you have not worked. A room not in use is a drain on her resources. Others have been dismissed for as much."

Mistress Ouish, though now blind and close to death, was still the dominating presence at the House Without Clocks. Even Rawra Chin, who had not been employed at that establishment for five years, regarded the old woman with alloyed respect and fear. From his blatantly spurious sickbed, Foral Yatt spoke again.

"You are right. If no work is done here tonight, it will be the worse for me."

He raised his lowered lids and stared directly into Rawra Chin's eyes. He smiled, knowing that to smile altered nothing between them. The masquerade was accepted by mutual consent. His voice dry and measured, he continued.

"That is why you must do my work for me."

It was as if there were some sudden dysfunction within Rawra Chin's mind that rendered Her unable to glean any sense from Foral Yatt's words. "that," "must," "do," "work"—all of these sounded alien, so that She was almost convinced that the actor had coined them upon the spot. She ran the sentence through Her head again and again. "That is why you must do my work for me." "That is why you must do my work for me." What did it mean?

And then, recovering from the shock of the utterance, She knew.

She shook Her head and in Her horror still had room to be surprised by the absence of soft hair swinging against Her neck. Barely audibly, She said "No," but it didn't mean "I will not." It meant "Please don't."

But he did.

Donna Blerot took Her hand (His hand?) and pulled it up beneath the fur tent so that it came to rest upon the dampness between the disfigured woman's thick legs. Beneath her single outer garment the dame was naked, flesh damp and solid like dough.

Later, burying Herself in the woman's body as Donna Blerot sprawled back across the table, gasping noiselessly like a fish upon a slab, Rawra Chin looked down at her and saw the abyss. The bell of gray fur had ridden up to reveal the body beneath, so that it now covered Donna Blerot's face, birthmark and all. For a lurching instant the woman looked like a drowned thing washed up on the coastline of the Sea of Luck, a sheet already covering the puffy, fish-eaten face.

Fighting nausea, Rawra Chin shifted Her glance so that it came to rest upon Her own body, luminous with sweat, plunging mechanically forward, jerking back, thrusting and withdrawing like a gauntlet-maniken worked by the hand of another. She regarded the jutting hardness that grew from Her own loins and wondered how it was that She could be doing this thing. She felt no desire, no lust for the deaf woman and her bucking, heaving desperation. She felt nothing but shame and horror. How could Her body sustain such ardor in the face of that abomination?

Later still, Donna Blerot kissed Rawra Chin and left, closing the pale yellow door behind her. The performer sat naked in one of the wooden chairs, elbows resting upon the tabletop before Her, face concealed behind Her hands as if behind the slammed doors of a church. The memory of the matron's kiss was still thick about Her lips. It had seemed as if a fat and bitter mollusk were attempting to crawl into Her mouth, leaving its glistening saliva trail across her chin. This imagery slithered out of Her mind and down Her throat, from whence it dropped into Her stomach. There was a faint, warning spasm and Rawra Chin tortured Herself with an image of their hastily devoured meal from earlier that evening. The gelatinous, half-melted skirt of fat trailing from the gray-pink fingers of meat...

Struggling silently to keep from vomiting, She did not hear Foral Yatt leave his bedchamber until he was standing just beside Her.

"There. Was that so bad?"

Startled by his voice, Rawra Chin moved one hand so that only half of Her face remained concealed, and opened Her eyes. She was looking down at the floor, and She could see nothing of Foral Yatt above the knee without moving Her head, which seemed an unendurable prospect.

His feet were as white as the flesh of almonds.

Fixed to each of the toenails was a tiny mirror. Suspended beneath the surface of ten miniature, glittering pools, Rawra Chin's reflections stared back at Her, insects drowning in quicksilver.

Rising unsteadily from Her seat and pushing past Foral Yatt, Rawra Chin staggered to that chamber set aside for bathing and the performance of one's toilet. Lava rose in Her throat, flooding Her mouth, and She was sobbing as She emptied herself noisily into a chipped and yellowed handbasin. Drained, She gagged upon emptiness until the convulsions in Her gut subsided, and then raised Her head to look at the room about Her through a quivering lens of tears.

Something caught Her eye, a green blur twinkling from atop the chest where Foral Yatt kept his soaps and perfumes and oils. Rawra Chin wiped Her eyes with the blunt edge of one hand and tried to focus upon the distracting blot of emerald. It was a fixed point on which to anchor Her perceptions, still reeling in the wake of Her nausea. Gradually, the object swam into definition against the damp gloom of the washroom.

Tiny glass sockets stared at Her, unblinking. Behind them, within the translucent green brainpan, unguessable dreams marinated within cerebral juices that smelled of licorice.

Rawra Chin stared at the skull full of poison. It stared back at Her, its gaze concealing nothing.

Time passed in the House Without Clocks.

On the eighteenth night following Her arrival, Rawra Chin fell to the darkness. That which had only licked and tasted Her now distended its jaws and took Her at a bite.

She was drunk, although it would have happened had this not been the case. Miserable over the dinner table, She had taken an excess of wine in the hope of numbing the pangs of self-loathing. The alcohol served only to muddy Her anxieties, making them slippery, more difficult to apprehend. She stood framed in the open doorway with one hand upon the pale yellow wood, looking out at the deserted courtyard, drinking great ragged lungfuls of autumn air. It did nothing to still the buzzing the droned inside Her head, a dismal hive somewhere between her ears.

Gazing at the indifferent black flagstones, She understood that She must leave. Leave Foral Yatt. Leave at once and return to the soothing babble of Her wardrobe boys, the comforting dreariness of committing endless lines to Her memory. If She did not go immediately, She would be trapped forever, crushed beneath the hulking farm wagon of circumstance, screaming for someone to brush away the flies. If She did not go immediately...

From the chambers behind Her, Foral Yatt called her name.

She looked up from the wide obsidian pond, there reared the archway, with Liavek beyond it.

A note of mounting impatience discernible in his voice, Foral Yatt called again.

She turned and walked back into the house, closing the pale yellow door behind Her.

He was in the bedchamber, as had become customary since the evening when Rawra Chin had been call upon to service Donna Blerot, Her first knowledge of a woman. She supposed that Foral Yatt had summoned Her to order a repetition of that occasion, and for an instant She savored a fantasy of refusal, but for not longer than that.

"My love? Would you light the lantern for me? It is so dark in here."

Foral Yatt's voice, altering since Rawra Chin's arrival in that place, had moved into another stage of its metamorphosis. softened to a deep velvet, it seduced rather than commanded.

Her fingers struggled with the flint for a second before the tinder caught, and then She lifted the flame to the wick of the lantern. A bubble of sulfurous yellow light expanded and contracted within the chamber, wavering until the flame grew still and its light clear. Rawra Chin turned from the lamp, white-hot maggots engraved upon Her retinas by the brilliance She had brought into being.

Foral Yatt lay upon his side on top of the patchwork counterpane, supporting himself upon one elbow, fingertips lost in the tight blond curls at his temples. A wide band of blue cosmetic color ran in a diagonal line across his face, overlaying the left side of his brow, sweeping down across the left eye, the bridge of the nose, the right cheek. A narrower band of red, little more than a single brushstroke, followed its upper edge over the ridges and hollows of his smooth, sculpted features, terminating beneath the right ear.

He was wearing one of Her costumes.

It was a gown, long and violet, gathered in extravagant ruffs at the shoulders so that the arms were bare. The collar was high, reaching to the point just above the bulge in Foral Yatt's throat, and below that the material was solid and opaque until it reached a demarcation line just beneath the breastbone. From there, the dress seemed to have been slashed into long strips that trailed down to the ankles, every second violet ribbon having been cut away and replaced by a panel of coral pink twine, knotted into snowflake patterns through which the skin beneath was visible.

There were mirrors upon his toes and fingers.

Entering through a chink in the wall with a sound like a child blowing across the neck of a narrow jar, a breeze disturbed the perfumed air and caused the lantern flame to stutter. For a moment, armies of light and shadow rushed back and forth in quickfire border disputes. The shadows gathered within Foral Yatt's eye sockets seemed to flow across his cheek like an overspill of tar before shrinking back to pool beneath the overhang of his brow. He smiled up at Her through lips fastidiously stained a rich indigo.

"I had to come back. I couldn't just leave you here."

The second word in each sentence was stressed in a lush and affected manner, so that even as Rawra Chin struggled to make sense of the actor's words, so too was She striving to identify that quirk of inflection, maddeningly familiar and yet beyond the grasp of her recall.

"But...what do you mean? You haven't been anywhere. You..."

Rawra Chin could feel something bearing down upon Her, coming toward Her with a hideous speed that froze the will and made evasion unthinkable. It was like stories She had heard concerning eclipses when men would see the giant moonshadow rushing toward them across the land a vast planet of darkness rolling over the tiny fields and pastures with a speed that was only comparable to itself. Standing there in the scented chamber, She understood their terror. The shadow-world was almost upon Her. Another moment and She would be crushed beneath its endless, inescapable mass. From the bed, Foral Yatt spoke again. The pattern of emphasis within his speech continued to dance just beyond the fringes of recognition, mocking and unattainable.

"I left you. Don't you remember? I left you because it was so important to me that people should know my name. I know it must have seemed unfair to you, but you were only ordinary, and I am a special creature. I have something rare in me, a unique charm that men have not words to describe, and though I loved you deeply, deeply, it was my duty to expose the treasure that I am to the world and all its people. Surely this is not beyond your comprehension?"

Quite suddenly, Rawra Chin knew where She had heard the voice that Foral Yatt was using. The dark planet crashed upon Her, and She was lost.

"But all of that is done with now. Now, people everywhere know my name and are drawn like moths to the fire within me, whose nature only I can put a name to. Now I am complete, and I am free to love you once more. I adore you. I worship you. I love you, love you more than anything in the world save for celebrity. But..."

The parody was unspeakably vicious, undeniably

accurate. Having identified the voice, Rawra Chin could do nothing more than accept the cruel mirror-image of the face that accompanied it. Nailed by the black weight of a phantom moon, She could only watch as Foral Yatt exposed all the conceits, the inanities, the small evasions that were the components of Her existence. The young man lounged upon the bed, touching a shimmering constellation of fingertips to the blue of his lower lip in a pantomime of anxiety and indecision. Looking up at Rawra Chin, his long lashes flashed an urgent semaphore pleading for sympathy while his jaw trembled beneath the burden of the words unspoken in the mouth above. Finally, when he had drawn out his melodramatic hesitation to the snapping-point of absurdity, the words spilled out in a breathless cascade.

"...but do you still love me?"

He paused, blinking twice.

"Despite what I did to you?"

In one corner of the room the idiot child began to blow across the slender neck of its jar, and the patterns of light and shade within the chamber convulsed. Rawra Chin, adrift upon a lurching ocean of nightmare, heard a voice speak in the distance.

"Is there a lizard asleep within the ball?"

The voice was so deep and masculine that She assumed it must belong to Foral Yatt, except that Foral Yatt's voice wasn't like that anymore. Whose, then, could it be? When the answer came, Her senses were too brutalized to ring with more than the dullest peal of despair. It was Her voice. Of course it was Her voice.

On the bed, Foral Yatt smiled and flopped languidly onto his back. The smile he wore belonged to Foral Yatt rather than to his grotesque and pointed lampoon of Rawra Chin, but when he spoke it was with Her accents.

"Perhaps I am a ball. Perhaps the unfathomable quality that men perceive in me is a lizard, coiled within me, its material reality questionable, its effects upon the mind undisputed."

Their eyes were locked, their awareness of each other fixed in that moment of mutual understanding that has always existed between snakes and rabbits. Licking his indigo lips, Foral Yatt luxuriated in the taste of the long instant preceding the stroke of grace.

"Shall I tell you the name of my lizard? Shall I tell you name of that thing that makes me vulnerable, makes me loved, worshiped, celebrated?"

Knowing the answer already, Rawra Chin shook Her head violently from side to side, but was unable to make the slightest sound.

"Guilt."

There. It had been said. He knew. The lantern flame quivered. The shadows charged and then fell back, regrouping for their next assault.

"You see, it is vital to what I am. It is the hurt that

drives me, and without it I am nothing. Oh, my love, I feel so ashamed of all the misery that I have brought you."

Standing at the foot of the bed, swaying, the wine of their evening repast now bitter in Her belly, Rawra Chin became confused as the layers of meaning began to fold in upon each other, blossoming into new shapes like a toy of artfully creased paper. Was Foral Yatt describing feelings of his own or mimicking those agonies that he perceived in Her? Did he genuinely feel remorse for the venomous charade that he had perpetrated? At the center of the fear and confusion that tore through Rawra Chin like a hurricane, a nugget of resentment began to form, cold and bright in the still heart of the cyclone.

How dare he apologize? How dare he plead for understanding after this insufferable pageant of debasement? The anger grew within Rawra Chin as She gazed icily down at the figure upon the bed, the yielding and defenseless line of the body beneath the slatted violet gown gradually becoming as infuriating as the wheedling of that unbearable little-girl voice.

"Can you forgive me? Oh, my love, you seem so stern. How thoughtless I was to injure you in such a dreadful, careless fashion."

Foral Yatt sat up and reached toward Rawra Chin with imploring arms, pale as they emerged like swans' necks from the ruffs at the actor's shoulders. His eyes pleaded for release from the apparent agonies of self-flagellation that he was enduring, and his blue lips mouthed inaudible half-words of explanation and apology, puckering as if for a kiss of absolution.

With as much force as She could muster, Rawra Chin struck him across the mouth with the back of Her hand, smearing the blue lip dye over his cheek and Her knuckle.

The dry smack of the blow and the bark of pain from the actor rebounded back at them from the cold stone of the walls. Foral Yatt fell back, covering his face and rolling onto his side so that he lay curled upon the patchwork with his back to Rawra Chin.

Struck suddenly by the sight of his curving spine, visible through the disheveled violet fringes of his gown, Rawra Chin found that the anger in Her heart was matched by a sudden pressure at Her loins as a burgeoning erection reared against the restricting hide of Her ash-gray breeches. On the bed, Foral Yatt nursed his mouth and began to weep. Almost of their own volition, fingers that felt suddenly numb and overlarge moved toward the knot in Her rope belt, where it pressed in a hard fist of hemp against Rawra Chin's stomach.

She raped him twice, brutally, and there was no pleasure in it.

When it was done, She understood the damage that She had done to Herself and began to sob noiselessly, in the way that men do, sitting there upon the edge of the counterpane with Her shoulders shuddering in silence. Foral Yatt lay on the bed behind her, staring at the far wall. Rawra Chin's seed had dried in a small, irregular oval on the plucked alabaster flesh above his right knee, a tight puckering of the skin beneath the thin, clear varnish. He picked at it absently with mirrored nails and said nothing.

The wick of the lantern grew shorter, until finally it guttered and died. Thus could the passage of hours be measured, there in the House Without Clocks.

"I had no right. No right to treat you like that..."
"Please. It doesn't matter."
"Will you stay? Will you stay here with me?"
"I can't."
"But...what am I to do if you go? There is no reason for you to leave."
"There's my work. My work and my career."
"But what about me? You're leaving me trapped here, don't you see? I'll never get away now. Please. I'll do anything you want, but don't leave me here."
"You should have thought of that before you took your revenge."
"Oh, please, I said that I was sorry. Can't you think of what we were to each other and forgive me?"
"It's too late, my love. It's far too late."
"I won't let you go. I won't let us be separated

again."

"Please. I don't want a scene. What happened last time was so embarrassing."

"Oh, don't worry. I won't make any fuss at all."

"Good. Now, I must send one of the House-waifs to order my carriage for the morning and arrange to have my wardrobe moved back to the lodging house."

"Won't you leave me anything? Please. Let me keep the violet gown."

"No."

"Don't you see what you're doing to me? You're taking away everything! How has this happened?"

"Don't be naïve. We are in the City of Luck."

"Here, you speak to me of luck? I am no longer sure that luck exists. Is there luck, or is there only circumstance without form or pattern, a senseless wave that obliterates all before it?"

"Is there a lizard asleep within the ball?"

Seated upon her balcony, absently chewing the anemic blue flowers she had plucked from her window garden, Som-Som regarded the courtyard of the House Without Clocks.

A carriage had arrived outside the curving walls with the first shafts of dawn, some short while ago. The half-masked woman had realized that Rawra Chin must be leaving the House to return to Her fabulous existence in the world beyond its seven variegated portals.

Since Rawra Chin had originally spoken of Her stay at the House in terms of months rather than weeks, Som-Som supposed that it was the dark undercurrents flowing between Her and Foral Yatt that had prompted this unannounced departure. She wondered if the performer would call upon her to say goodbye before She left, and felt a pang of sadness at the thought of their separation.

Countering this regret, there was a tremendous relief. Som-Som was glad that Rawra Chin had not allowed Herself to become a prisoner of the terrible gravity that the House possessed, and for this reason alone she hoped that luck would take the performer far beyond those walls that curved like gray, embracing arms.

The sound of the pale yellow door opening was jewel-sharp in the silent morning, and Som-Som leaned out from her balcony a little to watch the elegant, crimson-bandaged figure step out onto the cold black flagstones, where the chill of the night had left a faint dusting of frost.

To Som-Som, who had not enjoyed the perception of depth since her ninth year, it seemed that a self-propelling droplet of blood had leaked from a pale yellow gash in the skin of the House to roll across the frost-flecked black disk of the courtyard, trickling slowly toward the arch on the opposite side. Occasionally, a two-dimensional white hand would become visible, depending upon the perspective, a cream petal bobbing briefly to the surface of the red blot before vanishing again.

As the bead of crimson progressed across the yard, it became something that a person without her affliction would recognize as a human being. The figure paused at a point halfway across the courtyard and turned, tilting back its head to gaze directly at Som-Som, as if it had been aware of the half-masked woman's scrutiny since first setting foot outside the pale yellow door. From out of the redness, a face swam into view.

Foral Yatt stared up into Som-Som's eyes, both the one that blinked and the one that could not.

His expression seemed furtive for an instant, tinged with a guilt that Som-Som found disturbingly familiar, and then he smiled. Long seconds passed unrecorded while their eyes remained locked, and then he turned and continued across the wide circle of jet, passing out through the high stone archway.

After a moment there came the sound of reins snapping, followed by a rattle of hoof upon cobblestone as the carriage horses roused themselves and cantered off down the winding thoroughfares of Liavek, where the scent of a hundred simmering breakfasts hung reassuringly between the huddled buildings.

Som-Som sat motionless upon her balcony, her gaze still fixed upon the point where Foral Yatt had stood when he turned and looked at her. His smile remained there, an afterimage in her mind's eye. It was a smile of a type that Som-Som had seen before, and which she recognized instantly.

It was a wizard's smile. It was the expression of a luck-shaper who had finally achieved a satisfaction long postponed. For an unquantifiable time, Som-Som did not move. A blank expression was frozen onto her face so that those divided features regained a semblance of unity, the living half transformed to porcelain by her bewilderment.

Standing suddenly, she upset her chair so that it toppled to the balcony floor behind her. She moved rapidly, with an odd jerkiness. All of the training and discipline that had disguised her difficulties of locomotion were cast aside as she ran down the narrow wooden steps and across the rounded yard.

The pale yellow door was not locked.

Rawra Chin was seated at the table, rigid and upright in one of the straight-backed chairs. She seemed to be staring at two objects that rested on the white wood of the tabletop, barely distinct in the smoky dawn light. Approaching the table, Som-Som peered closer, squinting the eye that still possessed the ability to do so.

One of the objects was a plain copper ball that meant nothing to her. The other item seemed more like an egg with the top cleanly sliced off.

Except that it was green.

Except that it had empty, staring sockets and a lipless smile.

She noticed the odor of licorice at the same moment that she realized Rawra Chin had not breathed since her arrival in the chamber.

It was not a physical horror that propelled Som-Som backward through the pale yellow door, gasping and stumbling, shoved out into the courtyard by the immensity of what lay within. Neither was it an aversion to the presence of the dead. The whore of sorcerers is witness to worse things than simple mortality during the course of her service, and suicides at the House Without Clocks were frequent enough to be unremarkable. Certainly too frequent to engender so violent a reaction in one whose customers had, upon occasion, transformed into beings of a different species or entities of churning white vapor at the moment of their greatest pleasure.

Neither was it entirely a horror that preyed upon the mind, nor wholly a revulsion of the spirit. It had no shape, no dimension at all that she could grasp, and that was the fullest horror of it. A monstrous crime had been committed, an atrocity of appalling magnitude and scale that somehow remained both abstract and intangible. Having no perceivable edges, its monstrosity was thus infinite, and it was this that sent Som-Som reeling out backward into the cold, black courtyard.

She wanted to scream at the indifferent windows of the House Without Clocks, still shuttered against the morning light while those beyond enjoyed whatever sleep they had earned the previous evening. She wanted to cry out and wake the City of Luck itself, alerting it to this abomination, perpetrated while Liavek looked the other way, unsuspecting.

But of course, she could say nothing. The enormity of what had occurred remained locked within her, something scaly and cold and repugnant inside her mind, which could never be seen, never be touched or spoken of to another. Curled in the unreachable dark behind the porcelain mask it basked, beyond proof, beyond refute.

Hardly there at all.

FOREIGN PARTS

By Neil Gaiman

The VENEREAL DISEASE is disease contracted as a consequence of impure connexion. The fearful constitutional consequences which may result from this affection,— consequences, the fear of which may haunt the mind for years, which may taint the whole springs of health, and be transmitted to circulate in the young blood of innocent offspring,—are indeed terrible considerations, too terrible not to render the disease one of those which must unhesitatingly be placed under medical care.

                        Spencer Thomas, M.D., L.R.C.S. (Edin.)
                            A Dictionary of Domestic Medicine
                                and Household Surgery: 1882.

SIMON POWERS didn't like sex.

Not really.

He disliked having someone else in the same bed as himself; he suspected that he came too soon, he always felt uncomfortably that his performance was in some way being graded, like a driving test, or a practical examination.

He had got laid in college a few times, and once, three years ago, after the office New Year's party. But that had been that, and as far as Simon was concerned he was well out of it.

It occurred to him once, during a slack time at the office, that he would have liked to have lived in the days of Queen Victoria, where well brought up women were no more than resentful sex-dolls in the bedroom... they'd unlace their stays, loosen their petticoats (revealing pinkish-white flesh) then lie back and suffer the indignities of the carnal act—an indignity it would never even occur to them that they were meant to enjoy.

He filed it away for later, another masturbatory fantasy.

Simon masturbated a great deal. Every night—sometimes more than that, if he was unable to sleep. He could take as long, or as short, a time to climax as he wished. And in his mind, he had had them all. Film and television stars; women from the office; schoolgirls; the naked models who pouted from the crumpled pages of *Fiesta*; faceless slaves in chains, tanned boys with bodies like Greek gods...

Night after night they paraded in front of him.

It was safer that way.

In his mind.

And afterward he'd fall asleep, comfortable and safe in a world he controlled, and he'd sleep without dreaming. Or at least, he never remembered his dreams in the morning.

The morning it started he was woken by the radio ("two hundred killed and many others believed to be injured, and now over to Jack for the weather and traffic news ..."), dragged himself out of bed, and stumbled, bladder aching, into the bathroom.

He pulled up the toiled seat, and urinated. It felt like he was pissing needles. He needed to urinate again after breakfast—less painfully, since the flow was not as heavy—and three more times before lunch.

Each time it hurt.

He told himself that it couldn't be a venereal disease. That was something that other people got, and something (he thought of his last sexual encounter, three years in the past) that you got from other people. You couldn't really catch it from toilet seats, could you? Wasn't that just a joke?

Simon Powers was twenty-six, and he worked in a large London bank, in the securities division. He had few friends at work. His only real friend, Nick Lawrence, a lonely Canadian, had recently transferred to another branch, and Simon sat by himself in the staff canteen, staring out at the Docklands lego landscape, picking at a limp green salad.

Someone tapped him on the shoulder.

"Simon, I heard a good one today. Wanna hear?" Jim Jones was the office clown, a dark-haired, intense young man, who claimed he had a special pocket on his boxer shorts, for condoms.

"Um. Sure."

"Here you go. What's the collective noun for people who work in banks?"

"The what?"

"Collective noun. You know, like a flock of sheep, a pride of lions. Give up?"

Simon nodded.

"A wunch of bankers."

Simon must have looked puzzled, because Jim sighed and said, "Wunch of bankers. *Bunch* of *wankers*. God you're slow ..." then, spotting a group of young women at a far table, Jim straightened his tie, and carried his tray over to them.

He could hear Him telling his joke to the women, this time with added hand movements.

They all got it immediately.

Simon left his salad on the table, and went back to work.

That night he sat in his chair, in his bedsitter flat, with the television turned off, and he tried to remember what he knew about venereal diseases.

There was syphilis, that pocked your face and drove the Kings of England mad; gonorrhea—the Clap—a green oozing, and more madness; crabs, little pubic lice, which nested and itched (he inspected his pubic hairs through a magnifying glass, but nothing moved); AIDS, the eighties plague, a plea for clean needles and safer sexual habits (but what could be safer than a clean wank for one into a fresh handful of white tissues?); herpes, which had something to do with cold sores (he checked his lips in the mirror. They looked fine). That was all he knew.

And he went to bed, and fretted himself to sleep, without daring to masturbate.

That night he dreamed of tiny women with blank faces, walking in endless rows between gargantuan office blocks, like an army of soldier ants.

Simon did nothing about the pain for another two days. He hoped it would go away, or get better on its own. It didn't. It got worse. The pain continued for up to an hour after urination; his penis felt raw and bruised inside.

And on the third day, he phoned his doctor's surgery to make an appointment. He had dreaded having to tell the woman who answered the phone what the problem was, and so he was relieved, and perhaps just a little disappointed, when she didn't ask, but simply made an appointment for the following day.

He told his senior at the bank that he had a sore throat, and would need to see the doctor about it. He could feel his cheeks burn as he told her, but she did not remark on this, merely told him that that would be fine.

When he left her office he found that he was shaking.

It was a grey, wet day when he arrived at the doctor's surgery. There was no queue, and he went straight in to the doctor. Not his regular doctor, Simon was comforted to see. This was a young Pakistani, of about Simon's age, who interrupted Simon's stammered recitation of symptoms to ask: "Urinating more than usual, are we?"

Simon nodded.

"Any discharge?"

Simon shook his head.

"Right ho. I'd like you to take down your trousers, if you don't mind."

Simon took them down. The doctor peered at his penis. "You *do* have a discharge, you know," he said.

Simon did himself up again.

"Now, Mr. Powers, tell me, do you think it possible that you might have picked up from someone, a, uh, venereal disease?"

Simon shook his head vigorously. "I haven't had sex with anyone —" he had almost said 'anyone else,' "— in almost three years."

"No?" The doctor obviously didn't believe him. He smelled of exotic spices, and had the whitest teeth Simon had ever seen. "Well, you have either contracted gonorrhea or NSU. Probably NSU: Non Specific Urethritis. Which is less famous and less painful than gonorrhea, but it can be a bit of an old bastard to treat. You can get rid of gonorrhea with one big dose of antibiotics. Kills the bugger off ..." He clapped his hands, twice. Loudly. "Just like that."

"You don't know, than?"

"Which one it is? Good Lord no. I'm not even going to try to find out. I'm sending you to a special clinic, which takes care of all of that kind of thing. I'll give you a note to take with you." He pulled a pad of headed notepaper from a drawer. "What is you profession, Mr. Powers?"

"I work in a bank."

"A teller?"

"No." He shook his head. "I'm in securities. I clerk for two assistant managers." A thought occurred to him. "They don't have to know about this, do they?"

The doctor looked shocked. "Good gracious no."

He wrote a note, in a careful, round handwriting, stating that Simon Powers, age 26, had something that was probably NSU. He had a discharge. Said he had had no sex for three years. In discomfort. Please could they let him know the results of the tests. He signed it with a squiggle. Then he handed Simon a card, with the address and phone number of the special clinic on it. "Here you are. This is where you go. Not to worry—happens to lots of people. See all the cards I have here? Not to worry—you'll soon be right as rain. Phone them when you get home and make an appointment."

Simon took the card, and stood to go.

"Don't worry, " said the doctor. "It won't prove difficult to treat."

Simon nodded, and tried to smile.

He opened the door to go out.

"And at any rate it's nothing really nasty, like

syphilis," said the doctor.

The two elderly women sitting outside in the hallway waiting area looked up delightedly at this fortuitous overheard, and stared hungrily at Simon as he walked away.

He wished he were dead.

On the pavement outside, waiting for the bus home, Simon thought: *I've* got a venereal disease. I've *got* a venereal disease I've got a *venereal disease*. Over and over, like a mantra.

He should toll a bell as he walked.

On the bus he tried not to get too close to his fellow passengers. He was certain they knew (couldn't they read the plague-marks on his face?); and at the same time he was ashamed he was forced to keep it a secret from them.

He got back to the flat and went straight into the bathroom, expecting to see a decayed horror-movie face, a rotting skull fuzzy with blue mold, staring back at him from the mirror. Instead he saw a pink-cheeked bank clerk in his mid-twenties, fair-haired, perfect-skinned.

He fumbled out his penis and scrutinized it with care. It was neither a gangrenous green nor a leprous white, but looked perfectly normal, except for the slightly swollen tip and the clear discharge that lubricated the hole. He realised that his white underpants had been stained across the crotch by the leak.

Simon felt angry with himself, and angrier with God for having given him a (say it—*dose of the clap*) obviously meant for someone else.

He masturbated that night, for the first time in four days.

He fantasized about a schoolgirl, in blue cotton panties, who changed into a policewoman, then two policewomen, then three.

It didn't hurt at all, until he climaxed; then he felt as if someone were pushing a switchblade through the inside of his cock. As if he were ejaculating a pincushion.

He began to cry then, in the darkness, but whether from the pain, or from some other reason, less easy to identify, even Simon was unsure.

That was the last time he masturbated.

■

The clinic was located in a dour Victorian hospital in central London. A young man in a white coat looked at Simon's card, and took his doctor's note, and told him to take a seat.

Simon sat down on an orange plastic chair, covered with brown cigarette burns.

He stared at the floor for a few minutes, Then, having exhausted that form of entertainment, he stared at the walls, and finally, having no other option, at the other people.

They were all male, thank God—women were on the next floor up—and there were more than a dozen of them:

The most comfortable were the macho building-site types, here for their seventeenth or seventieth time, looking rather pleased with themselves, as if whatever they had caught were proof of their virility; there were a few city gents, in ties and suits. One of them looked relaxed; he carried a mobile telephone. Another, hiding behind a Daily Telegraph, was blushing, embarrassed to be there; there were little men with wispy moustaches and tatty raincoats—newspaper sellers, perhaps, or retired teachers; a rotund oriental gentleman, who chain smoked filterless cigarettes, lighting each cigarette from the butt of the one before, so the flame never went out, but was transmitted from one dying cigarette to the next; in one corner sat a scared gay couple. Neither of them looked more than eighteen. This was obviously their first appointment as well, the way they kept glancing around. They were holding hands, white-knuckled and discreetly. They were terrified.

Simon felt comforted. He felt less alone.

"Mister Powers, please," said the man at the desk. Simon stood up, conscious that all eyes were upon him, that he'd been identified and named in front of all these people. A cheerful, red-haired doctor in a white coat was waiting.

"Follow me," he said.

They walked down some corridors, through a door (on which DR. *J BENHAM* was written in felt pen on a white sheet of paper cellotaped to the frosted glass), into a doctor's office.

"I'm Doctor Benham," said the doctor. He didn't offer to shake hands. "You have a note from your doctor?"

"I gave it to the man at the desk."

"Oh." Dr. Benham opened a file on the desk in front of him. There was computer-printout label on the side. It said:

REG'D 2 JLY 90. MALE. 90/00666.L
POWERS, SIMON, MR
BORN 12 OCT 63. SINGLE.

Benham read the note, looked at Simon's penis, and handed him a sheet of blue paper from the file. It had the same label stuck to the top.

"Take a seat in the corridor," he told him. "A nurse will collect you."

Simon waited in the corridor.

"They're all very fragile," said the sunburnt man sitting next to him, by accent a South African, or perhaps Zimbabwean. Colonial accent, at any rate.

"I'm sorry?"

"Very fragile. Venereal diseases. Think about it. You can catch a cold or flu simply by being in the same room as someone who's got it. Venereal diseases need warmth and moisture, and intimate contact."

Not mine, thought Simon, but he didn't say anything.

"You know what I'm dreading?" said the South African.

Simon shook his head.

"Telling my wife," said the man, and he fell silent.

A nurse came and took Simon away. She was young, and pretty, and he followed her into a cubicle. She took the blue slip of paper from him.

"Take off your jacket and roll up your right sleeve."

"My jacket?"

She sighed. "For the blood test."

"Oh."

The blood test was almost pleasant, compared to what came next.

"Take down your trousers," she told him. She had a marked Australian accent. His penis had shrunk, tightly pulled in on itself; it looked grey and wrinkled. He found himself wanting to tell her that it was normally much larger, but then she picked up a metal instrument with a wire loop at the end, and he wished it were even smaller. "Squeeze your penis at the base, and push forward a few times." He did so. She stuck the loop into the head of the penis and twisted it around inside. He winced at the pain. She smeared the discharge onto a glass slide. Then she pointed to a glass jar on a shelf.

"Can you urinate into that for me, please?"

"What, from here?"

She pursed her lips. Simon suspected that she had heard that hoke thirty times a day since she had been working there.

She went out of the cubicle and left him alone to pee.

Simon found it difficult to pee at the best of times, often having to wait around in toilets until all the people had gone. He envied men who could casually walk into toilets, unzip, and carry on cheerful conversations with their neighbors in the adjoining urinal, all the while showering the white porcelain with yellow urine. Often he couldn't do it at all.

He couldn't do it now.

The nurse came in again. "No luck? Not to worry. Take a seat back in the waiting room, and the doctor will call you in a minute."

"Well," said Dr. Benham. "You have NSU. Non Specific Urethritis."

Simon nodded, and then he said, "What does that mean?"

"It means you don't have gonorrhea, Mr. Powers."

"But I haven't had sex with, with anyone, for ..."

"Oh that's nothing to worry about. It can be a quite spontaneous disease—you need not, um, indulge, to pick it up." Benham reached into a desk drawer and pulled out a bottle of pills. "Take one of these four times a day, before meals. Stay off alcohol, no sex, and don't drink milk for a couple of hours after taking one. Got it?"

Simon grinned nervously.

"I'll see you next week. Make an appointment downstairs."

Downstairs they gave him a red card with his name on it and the time of his appointment. It also had a number on it: 90/00666.L.

Walking home in the rain, Simon paused outside a travel agent's. The poster in the window showed a beach in the sun, and three bronzed women in bikinis, sipping long drinks.

Simon had never been abroad.

Foreign places made him nervous.

As the week went on the pain went away; and four days later Simon found himself able to urinate without flinching.

Something else was happening, however.

It began as a tiny seed, which took root in his mind, and grew. He told Dr. Benham about it, on his next appointment.

Benham was puzzled.

"You're saying that you don't feel your penis is your own anymore, then, Mr. Powers?"

"That's right, doctor."

"I'm afraid I don't quite follow you. Is there some kind of loss of sensation?"

Simon could feel his penis inside his trousers, felt the sensation of cloth against flesh. In the darkness it began to stir.

"Not at all. I can feel everything like I always could. It's just that it feels ... well, different, I suppose. Like it isn't really part of me anymore. Like it ..." he paused, "... like it belongs to someone else."

Dr. Benham shook his head. "To answer your question, Mr. Powers, that isn't a symptom of NSU—although it's a perfectly valid psychological reaction for someone who had contracted it. A, uh, feeling of disgust with yourself, perhaps, which you've externalized as a rejection of your genitalia."

That sounds about right, thought Dr. Benham. He hoped he had got the jargon correct. He had never paid much attention to his psychology lectures or textbooks, which might explain why he was currently serving out a stint in a London VD clinic.

Powers looked a little soothed.

"I was just a bit worried, doctor, that's all." He chewed his lower lip. "Um, what exactly *is* NSU?"

Benham smiled, reassuringly. "Could be any one of a number of things. NSU is just our way of saying we don't know exactly what it is. 'Non specific,' you see. It's an infection, and it responds to antibiotics. Which reminds me ..." He opened a desk drawer, and took out a new week's supply.

"Make an appointment downstairs for next week.

No sex. No alcohol."

No sex? thought Simon. *Not bloody likely.*

But when he walked past the pretty Australian nurse, in the corridor, he felt his penis begin to stir again; begin to get warm, and to harden.

■

Benham saw Simon the following week. Tests showed he still had the disease.

Benham shrugged.

"It's not unusual for it to hang on for this long. You say you feel no discomfort?"

"No. None at all. And I haven't seen any discharge either."

Benham was tired, and a dull pain throbbed behind his left eye. He glanced down at the tests, in the folder. "You've still got it, I'm afraid."

Simon Powers shifted in his seat. He had large, watery blue eyes, and a pale, unhappy face. "What about the other thing, doctor?"

The doctor shook his head. "What other thing?"

"I *told* you," said Simon. "Last week. I *told* you. The feeling that my, um, my penis wasn't isn't *my* penis anymore."

Of course, thought Benham. It's *that* patient. There was never any way he could remember the procession of names and faces and penises, with their awkwardness, and their braggadocio, and their sweaty nervous smells, and their sad little diseases.

"Mm. What about it?"

"It's spreading, doctor. The whole lower half of my body feels like it's someone else's. My legs, and everything. I can *feel* them all right, and they go where I want them to go, but sometimes I get the feeling that if they wanted to go somewhere else—if they wanted to go walking off into the world—they could, and they'd take me with them."

"I wouldn't be able to do anything to stop it."

Benham shook his head. He hadn't really been listening. "We'll change your antibiotics. If the others haven't knocked this disease out by now, I'm sure these will. They'll probably get rid of this other feeling as well—it's probably just a side effect of the antibiotics."

The young man just stared at him.

Benham felt he should say something else. "Perhaps you should try to get out more," he said.

The young man stood up.

"Same time next week. No sex, no booze, no milk after the pills." The doctor recited his litany.

The young man walked away. Benham watched him carefully, but could see nothing strange about the way he walked.

■

On Saturday night, Dr. Jeremy Benham and his wife, Celia, attended a dinner party held by a professional colleague. Benham sat next to an American psychiatrist.

They began to talk, over the hors d'oeuvres.

"The trouble with telling folks you're a psychiatrist," said the psychiatrist, who was huge, bullet-headed, and looked like a merchant marine, "is you get to watch them trying to act normal for the rest of the evening." He chuckled, low and dirty.

He drank too much wine with his dinner.

After the coffee, when he couldn't think of anything else to say, he told the psychiatrist (whose name was Marshall, although he told Benham to call him Mike) what he could recall of Simon Powers' delusions.

Mike laughed. "Sounds fun. Maybe a tiny bit spooky. But nothing to worry about. Probably just a hallucination caused by a reaction to the antibiotics. Sounds a little like Capgras's Syndrome. You heard about that over here?"

Benham nodded, then thought, then said, "No." He poured himself another glass of wine, ignoring his wife's pursed lips and almost imperceptibly shaken head.

"Well, Capgras's Syndrome," said Mike, "is this funky delusion. Whole piece on it in the *Journal of American Psychiatry*, about five years back. Basically, it's where a person believes that the important people in his or her life—family members, workmates, parents, loved ones, whatever—have been replaced by—get this!—exact doubles.

"Doesn't apply to everyone they know. Just selected people. Often just one person in their life. No accompanying delusions, either. Just that one thing. Acutely emotionally disturbed people, with paranoid tendencies."

The psychiatrist picked his nose with his thumbnail. "I ran into a case myself, couple, two-three years back."

"Did you cure him?"

The psychiatrist gave Benham a sideways look, and grinned, showing all his teeth. "In psychiatry, doctor, unlike, perhaps, the world of sexually transmitted disease clinics, there is no such thing as a cure. There is only adjustment."

Benham sipped the red wine. Later it occurred to him that he would never have said what he said next, if it wasn't for the wine. Not aloud, anyway. "I don't suppose ..." he paused, remembering a film he had seen as a teenager. (Something about *bodysnatchers?*) "I don't suppose that anyone ever checked to see if those people *had* been removed and replaced by exact doubles ..."

Mike—Marshall—whatever—gave Benham a very funny look indeed, and turned around in his chair to talk to his neighbor on the other side.

Benham for his part carried on trying to act

normally (whatever that was) and failed miserably. He got very drunk indeed. Started muttering about 'fucking colonials,' and had a blazing row with his wife after the party was over, none of which were particularly normal occurrences.

∎

Benham's wife locked him out of their bedroom, after the argument.

He lay on the sofa downstairs, covered by a crumpled blanket, and masturbated into his underpants, hot seed spurting across his stomach.

In the small hours he was woken by a cold sensation around his loins.

He wiped himself off with his dress shirt, and returned to sleep.

∎

Simon was unable to masturbate.

He wanted to, but his hand wouldn't move. It lay beside him, healthy, fine; but it was as if he'd forgotten how to make it respond. Which was silly, wasn't it?

Wasn't it?

He began to sweat. It dripped from his face and forehead onto the white cotton sheets: but the rest of his body was dry.

Cell by cell something was reaching up inside him. It brushed his face, tenderly, like the kiss of a lover; it was licking his throat, breathing on his cheek. Touching him.

He had to get out of the bed. He couldn't get out of the bed.

He tried to scream, but his mouth wouldn't open. His larynx refused to vibrate.

Simon could still see the ceiling, lit by the lights of passing cars. The ceiling blurred: his eyes were still his own, and tears were oozing out of them, hot down his face, soaking the pillow.

They don't know what I've got, he thought. *They said I had what everyone else gets. But I didn't catch that. I've caught something different.*

Or maybe, he thought, as his vision clouded over and the darkness swallowed the last of Simon Powers, *it caught me.*

Soon after that, Simon got up, and washed, and inspected himself carefully in front of the bathroom mirror. Then he smiled, as if he liked what he saw.

■

Benham smiled. "I'm pleased to tell you," he said, "that I can give you a clean bill of health."

Simon Powers stretched in his seat, lazily, and nodded. "I feel terrific," he said.

He did look well, Benham thought. Glowing with health. He seemed taller as well. A very attractive young man, decided the doctor. "So, uh, no more of those feelings?"

"Feelings?"

"Those feelings you were telling me about. That your body didn't belong to you any more."

Simon waved a hand, gently, fanning his face. The cold weather had broken, and London was stewing in a sudden heatwave; it didn't feel like England any more.

Simon seemed amused.

"All of this body belongs to me, doctor. I'm certain of that."

Simon Powers (90/00666.L SINGLE. MALE) grinned like the world belonged to him as well.

The doctor watched him as he walked out of the surgery. He looked stronger, now; less fragile.

The next patient on Jeremy Benham's appointment card was a twenty-two year old boy. Benham was going to have to tell him he was HIV positive. *I hate this job*, he thought. *I need a holiday.*

He walked down the corridor to call the boy in, and pushed past Simon Powers, talking animatedly to a pretty young Australian nurse. "... it must be a lovely place," he was telling her. "I want to see it. I want to go everywhere. I want to meet *everyone*." He was resting a hand on her arm, and she was making no move to free herself from it.

Dr. Benham stopped beside them. He touched Simon on the shoulder. "Young man," he said. "Don't let me see you back here."

Simon Powers grinned. "You won't see me here again, Doctor," he said. "Not as such, anyway. I've packed in my job. I'm going around the world."

They shook hands. Powers' hand was warm, comfortable, and dry.

Benham walked away, but could not avoid hearing Simon Powers, still talking to the nurse.

"It's going to be so great," he was saying to her. Benham wondered if he was talking about sex, or world travel, or possibly, in some way, both.

"I'm going to have such *fun*," said Simon. "I'm loving it already."

Afterword

I wrote this story almost five years ago, and I did the final draft (a hasty coat of paint and some polyfilla in the nastiest cracks) yesterday.

In between those two events it sat in a filing cabinet with a number of other short stories, fragments, things—there's even a children's book in there somewhere. All of them dusty and most of them well forgotten.

I remember its genesis: reading an underground strip called *NSU* in *Street Comix*, drawn by (a quick phone call to Hunt Emerson has just revealed) someone called J. C. Moody, which was followed by a conversation with my friends Ian and Martyn (in whose Barbican flat I was staying that evening) during which they exchanged, with relish, anecdotes of their respective experiences in the VD clinics of old London town.

I wrote the story over the following week or so, and found myself unable to sell it.

The SF/horror mags wouldn't take it because they didn't like the sexual content; even the 'men's magazines' wouldn't take it because it dwelt on aspects of and consequences to sex which they would rather ignore.

It went into a drawer, only to be pulled out for the Milford SF Writer's conference/workshop in 1985.

This wasn't the story I took with me to the workshop, which was, rightly, and looking back on it, very graciously, ripped to tiny shreds, but we had some extra time on the Saturday after the five days of intensive lit-crit, and need some extra stories, and, rather diffidently, I showed them this one.

They liked it.

One of them, British author and anthologist Alex Stewart, liked it an awful lot, and when, about a year later, he signed a contract with New English Library to edit an anthology of sex-related SF/Horror stories (called *Sex in Space* at the time; it's just come out under the title *Arrows of Eros*, which personally I happen to think a far less catchy title), he offered it a home.

I said no.

Things had changed. In 1984 I had written a story about a venereal disease. The same story said different things in 1987. The story itself might now have changed, but the landscape around it had altered mightily.

I'm talking about AIDS here; and so, whether I had intended it or not, was the story.

If I was going to rewrite the story, I was going to have to take AIDS into account. And I couldn't. It was too big, too unknown, too hard to get a grip on. The ramifications seemed endless, and damn it, it was killing people. It still is.

Over the last few years I have heard two schools of

thought (or at least schools of bar-room conversation, which is not entirely the same thing) about AIDS: those who assumed that everything would carry on exactly the same as before; and those who knew everything had changed. Well, the dust hasn't settled yet. Many good people have died, and are still dying. Many, many others are HIV positive. And we've all learned a lot (I hope).

But the cultural landscape seems to have shifted once more, shifted to the point where I feel, if not comfortable, then less uncomfortable about taking the story out of the cabinet, and brushing it down, wiping the smudges off its face and sending it out to meet the nice people.

I could say that it's not a story about AIDS. But I'd be lying, at least in part.

However, on the whole I think it's mostly about loneliness, and identity, and, perhaps, it's about the joys of making your own way in the world...

Neil Gaiman
November 1989

FOUR POEMS

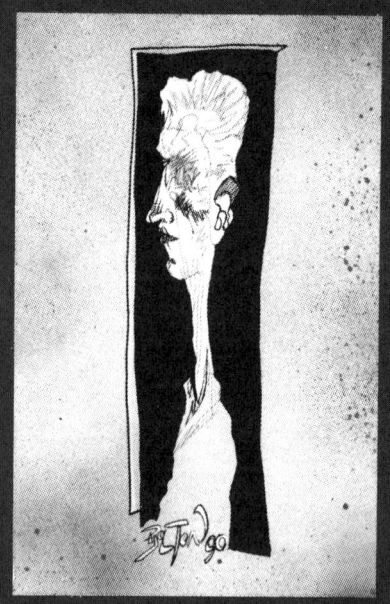

By Jon J Muth

The Storm

...We stood there in the road, watching, and it seems I fell into a momentary trance.

The sky darkens—blue clouds, almost black, are coming over from the south-southeast. The light burns green, slanting from the east, and the forested hills are suddenly beautiful: great, white sycamores reach out from the blue-black and burnt-orange forest like the pale arms of a drowning man. The colours are like an explosion: hot and fiery; a deep-laid dynamite charge bursting forth from roots buried beneath emerald-green grass—flying up and out of tree-fingertips into the air like arm-fulls of loose bloom. Gnarled old men stand beaten in rolled up shirt-sleeves and fedoras, rakes useless, hopelessly gathering the leaves as they swarm. Above us the thunderheads float, loaded and flashing with lightning. A widening patch of pale, churning, sky sends in the wind from ten miles away. We can see it coming at us like a violent, thrashing scythe; the cutting edge—a wave that passes, sending shock waves through the oak trees. The willows are in motion, bending and buckling like the sea. In the deafening roar of the world, the small stones, leaves and dust are blown needles against my face. Everything grows darker, more ominous. The sound is like a thousand steam engines, each one with its whistle blowing.

I pulled my collar up over my ears and ran...

(1986)

Faces

She stood till the water was still
and her reflection—pensive,
silk light hair
falling over her shoulder—
looked back at her.
She seemed to be trying to read the face
as she would the face of a stranger.
The face said nothing.
As sweet and meaningless as a warm spring day.
She pouted,
frowned, experimented with a smile.

I smiled back.

(1987)

Winter

Snow falls in slow circles
Diagonal darts from heaven touch your tongue
and dissolve
and plunge inward
and hurl downward
thousands of enormous dreams

Every atom is quiet
As though a finger were placed to the world's lips.

(1983–9)

In the Ghost's House

Curtains of slow-motion
lace and nightmares
wave to me from your windows
glittering
like ships on fire
I caress your beautiful, bruised house
wounded
and startling as a wolf in full-moon light

Adrift like fluid through darkness
a wind
made by a thousand angry
unseen creatures flying
tilts back my head
In the momentary silence
between your heartbeats
I can hear
the appalling speed, in space
beyond stars
of light

Reading no name
inscribed on the cool vellum of your body
I write a new book
before me, beneath me,
above me

thighs white
like wisdom
your eyes full of unlit wings in flight
your body sways
and drips
like the whisper of snowfall

A sweet warmness and wetness gleams,
undrying, across my own mouth

(1989)

A SHOT OF DAMN
AND A PACK OF HELLS

Ann Nocenti

THE RAIN FELL in fat sparse drops, a dull splatter. Carlos wrapped his leg around a pillow, listening to its idle talk. The tempo slowed, and he began listening to the thin silence between drops. He felt as if he was being fed, slowly, as in a Chinese water torture. Fed life and desire in thin slices that tasted of cardboard and peaches.

Above, the motel ceiling spread with water stains, and outside, the sun had been vanquished from a slate sky. Faintly, behind the wall of the next room, rose a weak laugh. Life, humid and sweaty, was as it ever is. Sometimes, if it wasn't for his craving for a cigarette, he'd never get out of bed.

There they were on the bed table, grinning a straight-toothed grimace, all twenty resting peacefully innocent in their perfect little flip-top box. He didn't even have to get out of bed. Carlos stretched for a match and wrapped his leg tighter around the pillow as he struck the flame.

It burns but good. Hot snake smoking down, peeks around curves, like a worrying tongue, testing. More, we want more, deeper. Tickling, cascading, spills in and fills the lungs' cups. Curl along the bottom and rise in soothing waves. Susserus trailing fingertips gently on pink interiors. Welcome. Rather fight than switch.

He stubbed it out, jammed in an ashtray spiked full of a dozen crooked white nails, and resigned to get out of bed. As always, his twenty minute efficient routine was completed to the second, tossed off with a final flick of comb through hair. Carlos opened his sample case, and neatly rearranged the rows of cigarette boxes, ten more samples for ten more cities. Ten more motels, ten more motel pillows.

One more for the road. He passed the time finishing his smoke by flipping through the sample booklet full of new advertising. Sports stars, speedy cars, vogueing stellar beauties, health and wealth, all floating in billboard heaven. Sell it with generic sex, no mention of cigarettes. A steady heartbeat of repetitive subliminal bullets depicting high lifestyle, the thin white smoking innocence of a cigarette held in graceful fingers eventually becomes part of the heavenly package. That was the art of the business these days. Sell a product without mentioning the product. Juxtapose, align, allude, but never say the word. Unspeakable products, highly marketable. Tastes good like a uh-uh-uhn should.

By now every cell was awake, aware, turning towards the warmth. The thin sensitive walls relaxed, porous, allowing the heat into the red river. The lazy meandering red river, with its thousand tributaries, brooks and thin streams. They mixed in and embraced their dear grey wispy friend. Blood and smoke, two serpents, entwined together to create new life. Kiss me, soft and grey.

Toothpaste, shampoo, razor out of the bathroom. Check under the bed for forgotten shoes, five dollars on the dresser for the maid, key hung back on the door. Carlos paused across from the dull chattering radio, waiting like a dog staring at an empty food bowl. He stood there through the sports, the foreign affairs, the commercials, not hearing a word. There was absolutely no reason he could think of to move on to the next town, the next motel. There, time to listen. thirty-five degrees, mixed clouds, showers, high forties. He snapped off the radio. Weather is always comforting, something to look forward to. Five minutes to the bus station. Carlos went out the door, returning briefly, for a book of Ramada Inn matches.

■

Suitcase in one hand, sample case in the other, he headed down the road, balanced as a pack horse. Town to town and rows of strangers. Buy my cigarettes. He might as well be a hobo hopping freight cars. Bus, town, bus, town, as endless as telephone wires stretching across a prairie. As nourishing as a thin, over-cooked soup, eaten because it's there.

Carlos watched a pretty woman approach the bus stop ahead of him. Black buckled boots and crimson stockings, long black coat and red leather gloves, tall furry black hat and long red hair. Carlos recalled a loose fact, about the poetess Sylvia Plath. She once declared that when she dressed in red and black it meant she was asking to be seduced. Carlos dug for his Ramada matches to light his cigarette. He'd stand near her, maybe catch her eye. He walked faster, drawing in smoke for confidence. Reach for a lucky today.

Tickling gently, warm tumbling smoke licked hungry lungs. The alert, intent cells were aching, ripe for it. Deep in their pink recesses now spotted with grey they hummed, with love. They were touched. Ready to creep, just a little, towards the warmth. They felt inspired to evolve into something new, something wonderfully devouring...for them to live the host body would have to be ravaged, willingly. This vessel will welcome the knife when it comes. Hungry, brave, and ready for the promised life. You've come a long way, baby.

She walked slowly, as if without destination, and he caught up with her easily. She hadn't noticed him yet. She just stared and smoked. The heavy tin sky, the wet streets, her red legs reflected in a water slick...it was a moment that would make a good ad, one his company would never buy.

She was intent on a man sitting along on the last bench. Carlos approached the bench and saw the man was dirty, a seasoned drunk. No, more than just a drunk. Carlos recognized something, a look in the vagabond's eyes, the look of a man who had searched and not liked what he'd found. Carlos noticed the others at the bus stop seemed familiar with him, as they avoided him like a toxicity. Carlos looked to the sky and wondered when the promised rain would fall.

■

Day in and out, everyone avoided the last bench at the bus stop, it was a bum's realm, Daniel's bench. He sat and watched the buses come and go, the crawling machines collecting and spilling humans, wondering if he'd make it through the next snow. The precious whiskey stung his lips, and he lost a few cheap drops down his chin.

Daniel waited till a few workers gathered. Sometimes he liked to be alone, sometimes he wanted the people to see him do it. He opened up his brown paper bag, and leaned back on the bench, his body forming a table. Slowly, he poured the bread crumbs over his chest, distributing the crumbs evenly and carefully, as if seeding a garden. They found niches in the many folds of his many coats.

The bravest were always first, or it was the hungriest. One pigeon, then three, soon a dozen.

They formed a fluttering, cooing blanket, hovering and hopping all over him. They were warm and friendly and pecked at his chest for the crumbs. Sometimes their sharp little beaks hurt him, but mostly they were gentle. Daniel felt the women turning away in disgust, praying for the bus to arrive soon.

When his friends were fed, they lifted away, one, three, then in a frenetic storm they were gone. Daniel sat up, satisfied. He liked to feed the pigeons. If you want something, give it. Daniel was always hungry.

Someone was on his bench, watching him. Daniel didn't like this, especially the way the stranger held his eyes, daring him. Like a dog, the stranger looked away first.

Daniel figured him for a traveling salesman, and was sure when the guy opened his briefcase, selected a pack out of the many samples, and offered a smoke. Together they lit up, Daniel making the stranger hold the match till it almost burned his fingers.

Soaked in smoke, bathed for years, given a new vitality. The cells were vibrating with apprehension, the metamorphosis was imminent. Cells shifted, new forms were created, abnormal shapes that nudged the next cell and sparked a creeping chain reaction. Wildfire, spreading geometrically. The multiplying cells hummed together, red to black, sensuous. When you're ripe, you know it.

 The woman approached the salesman and asked for a cigarette. She leaned in, and Daniel watched her heavy pendant, a silver crab, swing towards the man. Her accent was Eastern European, and weighty. She knew things. The salesman gave her one, lit it. She held his gaze. Deep in Daniel's brain he remembered something. His father, yelling advice at his sister: "Never hold a man's gaze steady, always look down and away." Again, it was the salesman that looked away first, like dogs do.
 Heads turned, bags were lifted, as the group noticed the approach of a slowing bus, its right light blinking. Daniel imagined the rest. These two finish sharing a cigarette, saying little, but their smoke drifts together and entwines. The salesman follows the girl

onto the bus. They sit together, and end up in the next town, at his hotel, lighting cigarettes with hotel matches. He knew the story. It was the only story, and it always started and ended somewhere. After that, you wanted no part of it.

    She walked away first, leading the way. Her face was that of an angel, her seasoned red legs said "not quite." The bus came and the bus went. She only looked back once. Daniel didn't ask questions. He just reached for another cigarette and offered the salesman a shot from his whiskey bottle. They both knew Carlos would be staying a while on the last bench at the bus stop, the bum's bench, exchanging shots for cigarettes. The hungry and the brave, everyone starts somewhere. The salesman took a draw on the whiskey and spat. "Damn! That's stiff."

    "Yeah, it's gutrot," shrugged Daniel. "I like it."

A CREATURE MOST DREADFUL

By Mark Evanier

No one could ever quite describe it because no one had the stomach to look straight at it. But Dennis could sure hear it, almost every night. And talk about a stench: It had that kind of chilling smell that reaches right up through your nose, grabs hold of your sinuses and tries to rip them out. A terrifying creature...and what it might do to you was beside the point; the mere fact of its existence was horror enough. It sat slobbering, feasting on all the life around it, giving out with a scream you could hear deep in your heart. And whenever you heard it, you couldn't help but wonder if you were really alive at all. Obviously, it had to be locked away.

Dennis Rowan was fourteen the first time he locked the creature away. That would have been in his parents' basement and he did it so skillfully, his folks never knew it was down there, not even when Dad went down to re-light the pilot on the heaters almost every week.

It was on a Tuesday in November, the culmination of three stormy months spent feuding with Louis Carlson at school. Exactly how it started, neither of them could ever explain. But they both knew that, when you're in a feud, all that matters is winning; doesn't matter what it's *about*. So Dennis spent those months hating Louis Carlson, plotting against him, fantasizing public humiliations for the guy, and didn't hear one word uttered by anyone in a teaching capacity. Not until one day in Health class.

The topic was puberty. As if any other topic could be discussed in a Health class packed with fourteen year old boys, as if any other topic existed on the planet. Dennis was mulling all that he could do to Carlson after school when Mr. Hansen, whose words otherwise went unheard, somehow managed to pierce the obsession barrier.

Said he, "When you get out of school, you're going to find that an awful lot of what goes on here isn't important. Things that matter like hell to you here will suddenly seem very trivial. And you'll be ashamed at how childish you were about them back then.

"It's a time (he went on) when your body is changing and you won't even understand all the changes. One day, somebody will call you jerko and for no reason at all, you'll just break out in tears. Just like that. No reason at all."

Dennis didn't have any perspective on being fourteen: you can't see the forest when you're one of the trees. But he instantly knew that Mr. Hansen, for once, was right. Which led to Dennis going straight home right after school and locking the creature away. For the first time.

He locked it in the basement again and again throughout teenage: the time Janalee Bingle refused to go out with him and he realized he didn't blame her. The time he won the state impromptu speaking championship and realized the award didn't make one bit of difference in his life. The time he broke out in tears during lunch, right there in front of everyone, and they were all staring and asking, "What are you crying about?" and he couldn't tell them because he didn't know. Except that he knew that, whatever had started it, he was now crying because everyone was staring at him and asking, "What are you crying about?" No one had even called him Jerko.

His parents never suspected the creature was down there. *There are some things you just can't tell your folks about.* If Dennis had told them about the creature down there, they would have panicked and felt they had to Do Something about it and they wouldn't have let him just lock it away and get on with his life.

So he didn't tell them. He just locked it away, happy

to have it penned up down there, no longer roaming about to interfere with his world. At times, he could even forget it was down there.

Except on "those" nights. It didn't happen all the time but, every now and then, lying wide awake in bed, he could hear it down there, its voice bellowing and echoing through the heating ducts into his room. An agonized scream it was and Dennis could only snuggle down under the blankets, repeating to himself that it was locked in down there, it couldn't get out, and that by morning, it would be silent again. It always worked that way but he could never quite get his stomach to rely on that.

As Dennis Rowan grew, so did the creature. For every inch Dennis grew, the creature put on six. Its teeth grew longer, as well. And sharper. And more determined to plunge themselves into Dennis' jugular, he knew. Now and again, he got a glimpse of it—and, every time, the creature was more horrible than he'd imagined. Bigger and with more scales and more blood puddling on the floor around it.

He kept on locking it in his parents' basement until the day he moved out. There was the big fight with Dad and that unfair suggestion—unspoken but there, nevertheless—that he was moving out because he didn't love his parents anymore.

Dennis entered the argument with every bit of logic and reason on his side: he was well past the age when all his friends had moved out of their parents' homes.

He was determined to win this one: he was well right and he knew it and he had all the evidence and there was no way he was going to let Dad pull rank and declare him wrong when he knew he had all the cards.

But then he looked at his Dad and, for the first time ever, he saw fear on his father's face—fear of being shut out of his son's life—and he suddenly knew that it had been there before, time and again. How could he not have seen it?

It was the first time he ever told his Dad he loved him. Then he packed up his battered Pontiac with books and clothes and everything he owned—and the creature—and moved to the new place he'd rented. First thing when he got there, he locked the creature away—amazed at how huge it had suddenly gotten—and then set to work to build a bookcase out of cinder blocks. There was no cellar but he managed to make do: he locked the creature in drawers, in closets, in his assigned storage chest in the carport…

For eight months, he was in love with a lady named Barbara. When it ended, it was painful—all the things he shouldn't have said, all the thing he should have known. Right after the last time he saw her, he locked the creature for a while in the kitchen cabinet—the one with the Kaiser Foil and the can opener—and never spoke the name Barbara again. He also had to give up Campbell's soup and stop wrapping his leftovers.

One night, shortly after, Dennis went out to a bar. He'd always had this fantasy of meeting a pretty girl in a bar, striking up a conversation and taking her back to his apartment for the night—something that had not been possible when he lived at home. It was a wonderful fantasy; one that got better and better with each lonely night's embellishments. Better and better it got until, much to his eventual disappointment, it finally happened. Her name was Lynda—with a "y," he was delighted to find out—and he took his time getting her back there, making the whole thing last longer, enjoying every second of it—

—until he got her home, got her into the bedroom and discovered he didn't much like Lynda, didn't find her as appealing in life as in the fantasy. Her interest in him did not extend much beyond tomorrow morning's breakfast and he was amazed at how that mattered to him. She said she was an actress but she certainly didn't know her lines, and, by not knowing them, managed to spoil the play for ever after.

That was the night he slept on the sofa in the living room. He had locked the creature in the bedroom with Lynda and she didn't even know it was there.

It was five years later that Dennis again dared to invite a young lady home but this one was different. Her name was Valerie and she was interested in more than just the one night.

In those five years, Dennis had only locked the

creature away twice, both times in the hall closet, where it remained relatively quiet. Now and than came a shriek or a moan but, for the most part, it kept to itself and caused him little trouble... amazing when you consider how large it had grown. By this time, it had started to resemble the Louisiana Purchase.

And then came Valerie. He met her at a party when she strolled up and asked him about the bandage on his hand.

"Oh, that?" he answered. "I got my cuff caught on the door lock on my car door and when I slammed the door shut, it yanked my hand into... well, you don't want to hear about it."

"Yes, I do," she said. And that was when he noticed her eyes. They were large and lovely and, best of all, they were focusing wholly on him.

She pointed to his bandage again. "Could I see your hand?"

"What's to see? It's just a yucky hand. I don't even like looking at it, myself."

"I'd like to see it," Valerie said.

"It's kind of messy," Dennis explained. "It's really scarred and sickening and it's kind of a pain to peel off the bandages and put them back."

"I'd like to see it," Valerie said. Clearly, there was no getting off this subject until she saw it.

So he peeled off the bandages and showed her. He didn't like doing it—didn't like seeing it, himself—but it seemed important at that moment. Later, he drover her home since she needed a ride and he decided that the other side of town wasn't *really* out of the way, even though he did live six blocks from the party. Ont he way, they stopped and bought more bandages. And condoms.

She was the first woman he was ever naked with. He'd taken his clothes off in front of a number of girls but she was the first woman he was ever naked with. Dennis couldn't tell her enough about his past, about his thoughts, about his fears, about his beliefs. Valerie wanted to hear every word of it and Dennis wanted to tell her.

So he started to tell her everything, starting with the story about the blue teddy bear that gave him his first nightmares. He told her about his dreams, about his problems, about his parents. They'd lived their lives for twenty-seven years apart so there was a lot of catching up to do. She, in turn, told him about her past, her pains, her private terrors. Her past was considerably darker than his. And would grow darker in the days that followed.

Eight weeks after he'd first met her, he had told her everything about himself except for the creatures and the story about Louis Carlson. Dennis knew it had to be love when he found himself telling her about the creature. He had never dreamed he would tell *anyone* about the creature.

Valerie listened. Than she said, "I want to see it."

"You can't see it," Dennis said, flustered that she would even suggest it. Why in God's name would a woman want to see *that*?

"It's part of your past, isn't it?"

"Yes."

"Then I want to see it."

Dennis felt trapped. He thought—but did not say aloud—"I never should have told you about it." He knew he couldn't say that to Valerie; it would just start another problem.

So he tried logic: "I locked it away for a reason. There's no point in letting it out."

He tried warmth: "Trust me. You think you want to see it, you say you want to see it. But you don't really want to see it."

He even tried emotion: "I know you want to see it but it would hurt *you* a lot if I open that door. Please don't make me do it."

Valerie didn't budge. She took his hand, kissed him lightly. "I've seen creatures before," she said. "You act like you're the only person in the world who's got one."

He stared at her. "I'm not?"

Valerie laughed. It was one of those "you're not serious?" laughs. Like he had just old her he had put a down payment on the Brooklyn Bridge. "You think you're the only person in the world with a creature

137

locked in your back hall—?"

"It's in the linen closet in the hall. I think." He noticed a pile of sheets, freshly folded from the laundry, sitting on the kitchen table. "Yes, it's in the linen closet. I couldn't put those away."

"Wherever it is. Dennis, believe me, everybody's got one. I've got one, my last boyfriend had one... everybody's got a creature."

Dennis was stunned. "You have a creature you lock away?"

"Well, no, I don't lock mine away. That's the difference between us. You lock yours away... you pretend it doesn't exist. I take mine with me everywhere I go."

Dennis glanced around. "Where is it?"

"You saw it. All those things I told you about:"

"That's not a creature," Dennis explained. "A creature is something you lock away—"

"Not necessarily."

"No, you lock it away. You slam the door on it and you get it out of your life."

"And then you have to worry about it getting loose," she said. "You live in constant fear of it getting out, of other people seeing it and blaming you for it and thinking less of you for it. That's why I take mine with me. So I don't have to worry about it getting loose."

Way too much happening here, Dennis thought; *I*

need time to think about this. "I'm sorry," he told her. "I can't show it to you. I just can't."

"Dennis," she said, her voice getting way too serious to suit Dennis, "I thought we had something happening here between us..."

"We do."

"Not if you won't let me see this creature that's such an important part of your life."

"Valerie," he pleaded with her. "I can't."

Valerie gathered up her belongings, put on her shoes and went home.

He wanted to stop her, wanted to say the words that would suddenly make everything all right. But such words, if they even existed, didn't find their way to his mouth at that moment. He waited for them and they never showed up. So Valerie went home.

The echo of the door slam was the only sound in Dennis' apartment for the next hour. Then it was slowly replaced by his sobbing. And a low moan from the linen closet.

"You don't understand," he finally told the spot on the sofa where she'd been sitting. "It's *my* creature. I control it. *Me, not you.* If it's going to get out, if someone else is going to see it, I have to be the one to decide. And I don't want to let it out—

"It isn't that I don't want you to see it. But I can't show it to you without looking at it myself. *And I don't want to look at it!*"

It all made perfect sense. But the couch couldn't answer him, couldn't tell him it understood.

And all this time, the creature was getting louder. And larger. And all the more sickening to look at.

The hours were far too long but way too short as Dennis wondered how he could make her understand. He had shown way too much of himself to Valerie to give up on her. For even if he could find another Valerie, another woman he cared about that way, he knew he couldn't bring himself to start all over with the story about the blue teddy bear again. Especially not after what had just happened. *If only I hadn't told her about the creature...*

Finally, he figured out what to do: she cared about him, she said. If she didn't, what he'd decided he should say to her wouldn't matter. But if she did, if there could ever be anything between them, he could make her understand with this simple explanation: "It will hurt me a lot to let it out. If you care about me, you won't ask me to do that."

That would do it. He would say that, she would say, "I *do* care about you, Dennis, so I'll never ask about the creature again," and they could get on with merging their lives.

Later that evening, after several halting attempts to dial all seven digits of her phone number, he made it. "It will hurt me a lot to let it out," he told Valerie. "If you care about me, you won't ask me to do that."

"I do care about you. That's why I have to see it."

No, no, no, he said. "It will *really* hurt me a lot to let it out. *Really hurt me.* If you care about me—*really* care about me—you won't ask me to do that."

"I understand that, Dennis. I swear to God, I understand you. But I have to see it."

"No, you *don't* understand. Listen to me. It will *really* hurt me to let it out. If you care about me, you won't ask me to let you see my creature."

"Dennis, I care about you. If I didn't care about you, I wouldn't give a damn about it. But I do—"

(It went that way for *hours.* Dennis didn't know it but the conversation was already over.)

Why, Dennis wondered, does it have to be so hard? It was all so simple in his mind, so painless, when no one intruded. Why couldn't Valerie accept that? Leaving well enough alone was obviously not among her skills. "It's my creature," Dennis found himself saying. "I know what happens if it gets out."

"It *will* get out," she told him. "You can't keep it locked in there forever. Eventually, it will get so big, so horrible that you won't be able to contain it."

"Yes, I can," Dennis yelled back. "I can keep it from ever getting out."

From Valerie, very quietly; "No, you can't"

Dennis was screaming now. "I can! I've kept it locked up all these years and I can keep it locked up for the rest of my life!"

There was a long pause. Maybe ten years. Finally, Valerie sighed and said, "I hope you and your creature are very happy together."

And she was gone. Again.

Dennis stared at the phone for a while, hoping that the dial tone would turn back into Valerie's voice Which didn't happen so he stared at it a little longer and it still didn't turn back into Valerie's voice. but that was okay; he was hearing her as he replayed the conversation again and again in his head...

"You can't keep it locked in there forever. Eventually, it will get so big, so horrible that you won't be able to contain it." She had said so many awful things but that was the worst of them. Because it was true. And Dennis knew it was true, knew it had always been true. It was at that moment that he realized he had always known he couldn't keep it locked up forever; that he was just buying time by not confronting it. " I should have it out when it was small enough to deal with," he said.

And that's when the creature broke free.

It started with a splintering sound—the linen closet door split right against the grain with one swipe of its claws. Then it reached out and ripped down the wall above and put a hairy foot, soaked in the blood of Dennis' worst fears, down on the floor. It was out.

Stumbling over his every thought, Dennis ran to try and force it back in, drive it back into some place that allowed Dennis to pretend it didn't exist. But the creature was far too large now for that; far too large to be locked anywhere in Dennis' apartment, for that matter. And loud: it had always been loud but, before, Dennis was the only one who heard it. Now it gave out with a scream, a loud and fervent cry broadcasting clearly for miles, down the block, across town, all the way to Dennis' folks' home and his high school and his junior high school and maybe even back east where Louis Carlson was now supposed to be living. They all heard it; all knew that Dennis' creature was loose, out in the world for all to see. You could even hear it over on Valerie's block.

Dennis forced himself to look at it. It was more horrible than he'd ever imagined.

It was thirty feet tall by now—how had he ever gotten it into that linen closet, anyway? Green and black and dripping blood and innards. It had teeth like razors, hundreds of them, and eyes that drilled for oil deep in your soul. Flecks of foam cascaded from its mouth, rolling down its fur, adding to a pool of stench and vomit all around. It looked like Hell. And smelled the part.

Dennis just stood there, letting its hot, piercing breath roll about him as a hurricane. As sickening, as destructive as it was, he had to look. It was as if his hindbrain had designed the most horrifying image for Dennis to look upon. Even the blue teddy bear in the creature's claws was frightening to gaze upon.

And now the creature was stalking forth, knocking down walls, unsettling furniture... smashing Dennis' cinderblock bookcase. The next day, all would be normal again and he knew it—in his head if not his stomach. But at just that moment, Dennis' entire apartment—his whole world—was destroyed before his eyes.

The creature stormed out into the street, out in front of everybody, displaying for the world to see twenty-seven years of Dennis Rowan's pains. Twenty-seven years of embarrassments and childish obsessions and wars that matter way too much at the time. Twenty-seven years of locking the old It away, feeding the creature with all the foolishness he'd known including most recently, the notion that you could keep the creature locked up.

Now it was out there: the creature, out there for the world to see. The thought of that had Dennis paralyzed; he just knelt there in what was left of his apartment, crying until long past there were tears left to cry. Dennis was fourteen again, left with no creature in the cupboard.

Eighty minutes later, there was a knock at the door—the same door that the creature, on its way out, had bitten right off its hinges and spat into the air. Somehow now though, it was back in place for Valerie to knock on.

When he heard the knock, Dennis knew it had to be

Valerie: who else would ever speak to him, now that the creature was loose?

She came in, cautiously, hesitantly, unsure of what she would find, what would be left. Most of Dennis seemed to be there.

Valerie said the words without which nothing else could be said, at least not right now. She said, "I'm sorry."

Dennis finally looked up at her.

"I'm sorry," she said. "You were right. It is your creature—"

"*Was* my creature," Dennis quietly corrected. "It's gone now. It's... out there... somewhere."

"It *was* your creature," she corrected. "And you were right. If you didn't want to look at it, I didn't have the right to force you to. It's just that... I knew..."

"So did I," he said. "That's how come it got big enough to get out."

There was a pause. A long one. Finally, Dennis said, "You shouldn't have done it."

Valerie smiled at him. "You're right. I shouldn't have." And then: "Hey, maybe if I keep learning stuff from you, I can start locking my creature away."

"Don't waste your time," he told her. "They always get out."

Smiles finally connected; that took a weight off Valerie. "You wanna go get something to eat?" she asked.

"No. But let's go anyway," Dennis answered. He looked around and found that most of his apartment was back where it was supposed to be. As she got him to his feet, he said, "I guess I'm lucky. Think of all the people in this world who never have a creature. They have to carry all that crap around with them forever."

"That's one of the things I was kind of hoping you could help me with," she said as Dennis locked the door behind him and they wander off for food. He wound up having a French Dip sandwich with a side of fries. She had the chopped vegetable salad. They talked about the weather, about a concert Dennis wanted to take her to, next week; about a car he was hoping to afford. He even started telling her about Louis Carlson and everything was fine.

And, oh yes: as they were eating, Dennis saw the creature running past the restaurant. By now, it was the size of a squirrel and getting smaller by the minute. And no one, particularly the two of them sitting there eating, gave a damn about it. By morning, Dennis thought, he might even be able to put the sheets away.

A SHORT TALE OF A YOUNG MAN WHO WOULD HAVE BEEN A PRIEST

By Charles Vess

AFTER DUSK WHEN THE SHADOWS ARE LONG and apt not to be false ones the old men of the village would gather together to tell their tales to whomever would listen. Many an evening the young ones of the village would sit, incredulous, listening to the tales those ancients would tell. But they would take special interest in the stories of the most ancient inhabitant of the village, in whose eyes they could see dim reflections of that which he spoke. Afterwards they would scurry home afraid of any mass of shadows or unnatural sounds, for the old men's tales would reach far into the night. At home their parents would scold them for wasting their time with empty tales and send them off to bed where they would dream rich dreams.

Now this is the story told by one of those old men

wise with the knowledge that comes with time. Perhaps it was told by that most ancient inhabitant; I don't remember. The years have been long and I now sit and tell my own tales—it doesn't matter, I have heard the tale many times since but the old telling was best.

In a kingdom very unlike the one you or I live in there was a beautiful garden. In this garden, when the sun had begun to set and shadows were long ribbons of blackness, there would fall a slow shower of umbrellas. No one knew where they came from, just that they were pleasing to look upon and that whoever kept one in his home would have an especially pleasant life. So the people of this distant kingdom revered these umbrellas past all other things.

After a great long time the temples and priests came into disuse for everyone had his or her own umbrella to offer prayers or sing psalms of praise to, so that there was no more need of those things.

Now there was a certain young man who had been studying diligently for a great many years to be a priest, so that when the time came that there was no need of his profession he was exceedingly angered. The youth determined that he should go to the source of these umbrellas and once there have discourse with their senders, explaining in all due humility that they had placed him as well as a great many other people out of their jobs. Furthermore they had eroded the moral fiber of his land, placing the souls of its inhabitants in danger of eternal damnation (for as everyone knew there was only one god, that being the one to whom he and his fellow priests supplicated). Surely, he thought, if they were intelligent beings they would understand his plight and rectify their grievous wrongdoing.

So early in the evening the youth crept into the garden, wearing the clothes of ordinary folk, so as not to cause suspicion among the other people gathered there.

They appeared first as small black dots in the distance, but slowly gained in colour and shape till everyone could recognize them as umbrellas. It was the people's custom to wait with bowed heads until the umbrellas had touched the ground and spun to a stop before the formal act of choosing was performed. But the youth who would be a priest did not wait. He quickly caught one of the umbrellas, folded it up and stuck it under his cloak before any of the others had raised their heads and prepared to receive their umbrellas. Only a few heads turned quizzically as he edged to the back of the crowd and made his way off into the deepening shadows.

Soon he was alone in one of the many deserted temples that now dotted the landscape. The would-be priest extended the brilliantly coloured object of his quest. It did, he decided, have a certain feeling to it that was alien to that which he deemed right and natural. He glowed in a feeling of purpose that had been vacant since his priesthood had lost its place in the people's lives.

Placing the umbrella in a dark recess of that temple he descended the one hundred and one ebony black steps to the Great Book of his priesthood. Before it he knelt and prayed mighty prayers of supplication, voicing his defiance of this new religion that had slowly crept into his land. The ritual over, he arose and in words unnatural to his lips (learned through extensive studies with the elders of his kind) spoke the incantations that broke the seals of their Great Book. Lore handed down generation after generation was stored in this Book and on one particular page was the answer to his question—one page among numberless pages told the secret of the umbrellas. If the youth was to wear nothing save a shirt and gloves soaked in a certain unnameable element and was to utter but four words written therein he could ascent the heavens in that umbrella which then would carry him through the skies to the land from which it came.

A smile of satisfaction lit his face as he ascended the one hundred and one ebony steps back to the umbrella. The still slightly damp shirt and gloves were held in one arm, and those four words he mumbled again and again under his breath. Taking the umbrella from his cache, he came to the roof of the temple. There he stripped down and donned the gloves and shirt, spoke the four words of power, and quickly sat down in the umbrella.

Suddenly the stars were much closer and the ice cold winds swept across his face. Far below the land in which he had been raised receded from view, replaced by vast snow-covered mountain ranges. All that long black night the would-be priest was swept through the air. In the morning, though, he slowly descended into a great city the like of which he had never seen. The umbrella tumbled to a stop and the youth hastily stood up. He was in the middle of a large, very crowded market place.

"Why, they look just like my own people; they do not look like gods at all!" he thought. The people nearby looked at him and his curious clothing; many of them laughed; several turned away casting sideward glances till they were out of sight. Bewildered, the youth prayed a silent prayed to his god but felt no lightening of the gloom that bore down on him.

From these people the youthful would-be priest quickly learned the truth and thus came to a sudden ending of his quest. The people of this city (which we will call Bethmoora, for its real name you would not believe), had a love for bright and colourful things, especially umbrellas. But they soon grew tired of them and wanted new ones. When they tired of them they let the strong winds that blew past their city carry them away, thinking that perhaps they would be found and enjoyed by others less fortunate than they. These people of Bethmoora found it immensely amusing that others in some far off land were willing to worship their umbrellas. They said that their god would frown upon such frivolous actions, and since he was the only true god the youth must forget such notions if he were to stay in their city.

So today if you were to walk through that fabulous city and approach the market place there you would see that young man, who had once desired to be a priest, no longer as young, but much more content. There he would be selling his umbrellas with many bright colours and strange designs, quite content to do so knowing what he knew.

JIZ AND BLOOD...
EVERYTHING MERGES
WITH THE NIGHT

By Stephen R. Bissette

H E STOOD BEFORE THE GRAVE, brooding. His belt was heavy with tools, the shovel held in white-knuckled hands. Rain hammered his brow, his shoulders, and ran in rivulets down his collar. A shitstorm in a world of shit, shit upon shit, and under his feet the biggest shit of them all.

Susan writhed beneath him, no longer enjoying their lovemaking. He couldn't stop now, so close to orgasm, though he slowed his rhythm as she brought her arm up over her eyes. That gesture of abandon, the feeling of her drying out even as he was about to spend, a sorrow that was dragging him down even as his passion peaked...

And suddenly, a face, from nowhere, unbidden,

glistening with animal madness before his eyes: an older man, his lips wet with spit, face swollen and veins distended, all rage and rape. It yowled into Michael's eyes as it threw itself at him full force—

It took him a while to realize she was gone. They hadn't slept together the night before—they hadn't been sleeping together for months, the truth be told, despite the decade they'd been husband and wife—and it wasn't until he noticed the remnants of her breakfast that he knew she'd gone.

Backtracking, there were clues, if only he'd been awake enough to notice them: his pants neatly folded at the foot of his—no, *their*—bed, where she had left them after taking the car keys from his pocket. The rumpled travel bags were gone from the corner in the bedroom where they had laid for so long, grey dustbunnies marking their passage. The bathroom's clammy dampness was evidence of her having showered before leaving, her brush, toothbrush, and personals missing, a wad of yellowed toilet paper still adrift in the bowl.

The open garage door and car-less gloom that yawned from it told the tale, had he looked out the bathroom window while taking a piss. He hadn't noticed because the piss was all that had mattered just then, easing his swollen bladder (distended with the runoff from last night's brews) and the raging, pointless erection he woke up with every morning.

But it was the kitchen that tipped her hand, the plate of half-eaten toast and already coagulated eggs that sat by the sink. She *never* ate breakfast, and it was this that stopped him in his tracks and set the alarm ringing dimly in the back of his skull.

He shuffled over to the table, already numb with the realization of it. She was gone, and he had no idea where to, or if she'd ever be back. Perhaps to one of her friends, or therapists, or one of the women-only retreats... none of which he had any way of tracing, as those aspects of her life had less and less to do with his—no, *their*—life as her melancholy and the black tide from her past had overwhelmed every waking and sleeping moment of each day. He glanced over to the phone, the notion of calling someone dashed as he noticed her address book was gone as well. Of course. She had stopped sharing that information with him weeks ago, after the argument that ended in violence. The memory of it brought the ache back into his healing fist.

He looked down at a piece of paper that lay there for him. His own name, followed by a dash of blue ink:

"Michael—"

And nothing more. His name, a slash: no more had to be said. It summed up affairs quite nicely, really.

—The face hung between them, twitching and

quivering, eyes glassy, the engorged tongue lolling with spasmodic release—

In a second, it was over, and Michael lay shivering and sobbing, curled like a fetus with his back to Susan. He couldn't remember pulling out of her, just the face, that damned face, and his gut turning with the barrage and its baggage. She rolled over, suddenly, and held him.

"Michael, what—"

"A...face...and I felt..." He took a ragged breath.

"...I was *raping* you..."

She tried to comfort him, but there was no consolation. They shivered, alone, together, in the dark.

He sat in front of the table, red-eyed and shaking from the cold (he was still only in his undershorts and slippers) and the roiling in his stomach. Spread before him were all the unfinished notes he had fished out of the garbage, the attempts she had made to explain. His name, a slash: an angry rant she couldn't complete because there was no focus for her shame and rage. His name, a slash: a tear-stained apology that ended in mid word, because there was nothing, ever, evereverever she had to apologize for. She had done no wrong, and yet everything was irrevocably wrong.

Name, slash: a plea, a promise, cut off before either could be made. Name, slash: Name, slash: one making his eyes sting with tears, another squeezing his chest like a fist. Name, slash: a spew of anger and desperation, with misspelled words cut into the paper like knives, the pen tip ripping through the virgin white surface, each barb ending with the name of the man who had turned their lives inside out, until it became a mantra, a litany of hatred, the last line simply repeating the name again and again and again:

"Ted."

Michael ran his fingers over the name carved in stone, the affectionate nickname mounted over a cherub's crying visage and the full name, "Theodore J. Solomon." It was the finest of granite, clearly the most expensive stone in this corner of the cemetery. Even in the darkness and rain, that much was evident. He ran his fingers over the name again, to be sure it was the right grave. *Had* to be sure, no doubt. His finger furrowed into the 'T,' listlessly over the 'E,' a talon by the time it had rimmed the 'D' for the fifth time.

Shifting the weight of his tool belt, he unzipped his pants and sent a steaming stream of piss over the letters.

By the time it had run its course down the gravestone and begun to seep into the soil, Michael had already begun to dig. And still, the rain fell, an endless rhythm...

The steady rhythm of her sewing machine sang through the floor, an instant barometer for her mood.

Even before they had decided to move in together, he had found the sound of Susan's sewing machine flawlessly conveyed her inner state, as if heart and machine were one. The machine would sing soft, steady, sure when she was happy, a choppy staccato when she was angry or upset. Between the two were countless, subtle differences he learned to read over the years. She could never hide her true feelings when she was working. The dance of her feet at the pedal, her hands pushing the fabric through the pumping needle and river of thread: it told all.

The day the memories began—not long before that face had erupted from their lovemaking—he had known something was wrong the moment he walked in the door, before her sobbing was audible. The machine stuttered, choked, sputtered in a feeble burst of stitches, and her scissors clattered to the floor. He cleared the stairs, two at a time, to find her bent over her work in tears.

"Susan..."

His hand touched her shoulder tentatively, and she wrenched away from it as if by reflex. She was as startled as he by her reaction, and after a moment's hesitation she allowed Michael to hold her, though she could not return the embrace.

After a long silence, she whispered, "I think I'm losing my mind, Michael."

And she told him, as best she could, about the first

memory, and let him hold her hand.

He had always been good with his hands. He dug with strong, rhythmic intensity, despite the throbbing in his head, the rain and the shifting of the dirt. It had been unbroken for years, and the rain was both a blessing and a curse, softening up the soil before the shovel blade bit into it, but hammering it into mud the moment it was exposed. None of it daunted him a bit, though; his rage, finally with a target in sight after so long, supped on the rain, the dirt, the mud, the sweat.

He turned the old dirt, bearing its secrets. The night and the storm were too good, too alive for it, but it would have to be exposed if the job were to be done; by dawn he would be finished, and the dirt and all it hid would be ravaged and then buried back up again.

Violation. That's what the face gave form to. Violation. The memory of it shook him still. It wasn't the cold rain or the wet clinging clothes that brought the goose pimples, it was that goddamnedmotherfuckinshitass face, hovering in his mind's eye.

Ted's face. Somehow, he'd gained a glimpse of Susan's memory that night...the monstrous face of her tormenter, her secret 'lover,' the man who had used her as often as he'd liked when she was a mere child. He was sure that it lay beneath the coffin lid, as black and bloated as he remembered; swollen with rot, not orgasm.

The shovel cut deeper into the dirt.

He had always been good with his hands, as had Susan. His hands earned their callouses and the deep-stained furrows of the grease monkey, though he was more than that now: he owned his own garage, and called his own shots. Hers were efficient as a seamstress, working out of her studio at home, and her handwriting was truly lovely: it had fueled his dreams when she wrote her first love note to him years before, and it broke his heart as it lay spread out before him on the table on the uncrumpled notes, giving a false sense of order to the chaos that had consumed her and swept her out the door as he had slept, stinking of beer, upstairs.

At first, when they were still friends and lovers, their hands—hers so willowy and supple, his coarse and thick, magically gentle when alone with hers—were as good as they could be. They fit together, their hands, and she slid her fingers into his own often and lovingly. she once told him that he was her strength, her 'rock,' and he had tightened his fingers over her own to seal that truth.

But they hadn't been good enough, loving enough, strong enough, somehow, and as the weight of years and deeds he'd had no part of broke her, she could draw no strength from him. His strength was male, and all that was male was somehow tainted and monstrous;

once the memories had come, all that was male was somehow poisoned by the bastard who had taught her what a man could do, if you were young enough, if you were helpless enough, if you were a little girl.

Michael's hands had become useless, raised only in anger or clenched into fists, holding a sweating bottle (or his swollen cock as he jerked off in the morning) as if it were a gearshift that could shift into the overdrive that sped him—*them*— away from the awful darkness. After the argument that drove the final wedge between them, he had raised his hand in violence—not to strike her, for he had never resorted to that. No, he had hammered at the walls and doors until his right hand exploded through glass, cutting tendons and scraping bone.

In the wake of that night Susan's hands became limp and often shaking, listless like a bird's broken wing. He still, occasionally, tried to hold them, but his grip was no longer returned: no trust, no strength to give or take. Her touch was tentative at best, and much—her work, her Michael, her own sex—was hardly touched at all.

They had been so good with their hands. If only they had been better with their heads, or their hearts, he thought now. Maybe if they had born children, an innocent male child, perhaps that might have changed things. If only they had been stronger, or more imaginative, perhaps there would have been a way to grasp the memories, tear them asunder, or away, or at least at bay long enough to keep their lives together.

Now the rage controlled his hands, and all he wanted to do was tear up the burrow the bastard hid within, pry open the lid, and rip the fucker's blackened heart out.
 The pit was shoulder deep, and still he dug. His hand had begun bleeding at some point, whether from the cuts reopening or another callous torn open, he didn't care. It hurt, but the pain only fueled his frenzy, digging until the shovel struck an unyielding object. The blow jolted his shoulders and tore his hands further, but it made no difference: this was it.
 The coffin.

Why couldn't it have just stayed buried, forever?
 The first memory had been fleeting, but it was the tactile immediacy of it that so frightened her: the weight, the smell of the big man, the pressure on her vitals, the involuntary gagging as something was forced into her mouth. And after the first memory, others: splinters, shards, splashes.
 Ted, in his car, picking her up. Ted, leering over her, oblivious to the pain he caused her as he sweated and shook. Ted, punishing her, forcing her legs apart, laughing as he pushed objects inside of her. Ted, a rope of saliva from his lips, lost in his perversion, treating her

like an object to be used and discarded at whim. Ted, speaking gibberish, biting her, telling her no one would believe.... Her mind had buried it deep, deep, but her very cells had remembered it, after all these long years. The color of a length of fabric, an odor of tobacco, Michael touching her nipples, the pumping of the sewing machine...anything, anytime, could bring another fragment of pain to the surface. Another memory. Another agony.

She told Michael all she could, until he turned away. Her therapist told him the rest, as Susan had asked: she couldn't bear the pain it caused him, as if *she* were to blame, as if it were here shame, breaking her—their—spirits. A hideous thing had come between them, and try as they might they could not define or contain it. It was too big, too filthy, and had been denied too long. Once it had been disintered it could not be buried again.

After clearing the mud away from the edges of the damned thing, he no longer needed the shovel. For a moment he stood on the lid, sizing up the coffin's parameters in the dim light of the flashlight: it seemed huge, and the lid along was no doubt a heavy burden of layered wood and cement and silk. Silk: why wrap a turd in silk? His anger flared as the lightening did, and he threw the shovel out of the pit, striking sparks as its blade kissed the gravestone.

"Anything could have sparked these memories. I can't tell you *why* they've surfaced *now*. It could have been anything, really...some little thing, probably. You see, she didn't *consciously* remember them, she'd buried them so deeply. It was as if it had never happened, or so her unconscious tried to make it seem."

The therapist spoke slowly to Michael, as if he were a child. He looked at her, unblinking, unsure of how much stock to put in this stranger's words. Good God, it was *Susan*, his wife, she was talking about. Why wasn't Susan telling him this?

"You must understand, it isn't you or your fault...she can't help what she's feeling now," the doctor said, looking away from him for only a moment. She paused and met his gaze again before speaking. "It isn't *you* she's afraid of, it's *him*—"

"But he's *dead*," Michael spat.

"Yes, he is. But it's *him, his* touch, *his* abuse...and right now, anything sexual..." she said, looking for some confirmation from Michael's slate eyes. For a moment he stared, stoney and defiant, before looking away. He wouldn't tell her she was right, or of the face. He was sure: *Ted's* face.

"She was sexually abused, and the scars—well, they aren't scars. They never healed. They're *wounds*, and they've reopened. I know it's been hard, but you have to understand that only *now* can the healing begin,

Michael." She reached to touch his hand for the first time.

"My God, sh— she was seven years old—" he whispered, and his vision blurred.

No. He wouldn't cry. Not now.

Michael dropped to his knees, teeth bared. His bloodied hand wiped the mud from the edge of the lid until it bared the top of a screw, gleaming like a maggot furrowed in rank meat.

He felt the tools in his belt until he found the pneumatic screwdriver. No doubt the lid would be heavy.

It was too great a burden, and yet he was to tell no one, least of all her parents, who had counted Ted as one of their closest friends.

Ted, the upstanding citizen. Member of the Knights of Columbus, a devout Catholic, respected realtor and town selectman. Ted the bachelor. Ted the ladies' man. Ted the bastard pedophile, the closet sadist, Ted the torturer of little girls. Ted the dead, six feet under, stiff and gone, wormfood, out of reach forever and forever, Amen.

Ted, who climbed into bed with them until they slept apart, whose lipless grin somehow replaced Michael's every kiss, who screamed in Michael's face at the moment of climax. Ted, who reached from the grave and ripped their marriage apart.

So long together, so strong, now splintering like rotted wood at the touch of a man long dead.

The wood splintered as Michael worked the screws out with the pneumatic screwdriver. The coffin hadn't been made to be opened: it had been designed to seal out the dirt, the vermin, the rain and rot and touch of time. At first, the damned thing had seemed inviolable, as if defying Michael to open if. The screws had been countersunk, but he'd dealt with harder jobs in the garage. The pneumatic screwdriver did its job. It was still a bitch. His hand bled freely now, the bandage flush with scarlet that spilled over as he flexed his hand and forced the screwdriver into action again, and again, and again.

When they did make love, she seemed to be barely there.

Then the gesture: her arm over her face, eyes buried in the crook of her elbow, as if to block him out. He tried to change, now gentler, now rougher, different foreplay or positions, but still she seemed aloof and distant at some unknown shift in mood during the play of sheets and flesh. Sometimes he would delight in her touching him like before, stroking him and guiding him into her…then, inevitably, the gesture. Her arm would cross her brow, nestle over her eyes, and she was gone, even as he thrust into her.

Than, that night, the face—HIS face—

The last screw rolled into the mud. By the time it sank from sight, Michael had already begun to pry the seal open with his crowbar.

In his mind's eye, he could almost see the bastard's face as the smell began to seep into his nostrils.

There was a certain comfort in the smell of gasoline and oil. The garage was rich with the odor, and Michael stood beside the wrecker in the dark and drank it in. In his hand was a map, with a route marked in red marker, leading to Susan's home town. He'd been there plenty of times over the decade, and thought he knew where the graveyard was. It was a small town, with just the one boneyard: there were plenty of graves, but he knew he'd find the one he was looking for in short order, rainstorm or no. The insanity of his plan overwhelmed him until his anger, bottomless and forever without a focal point—until *now*— reasserted itself. He strode to the wrecker and opened the door, tossing the map onto the tool belt and heavy-duty flashlights he'd already set on the passenger seat. The shovels were already in back, and he'd loaded the chains. He'd yank the fucker right out of the ground, if he had to.

Michael paused by the cab door, and then stepped back. This was his garage, his wrecker: it had kept him busy, kept food on their table, took care of him and Susan. It was the only anchor left to him now.

She had taken the car, and she was gone. There was some blessing in that, as he had feared she might take her own life in the past few weeks... she was gone, but at least alive. Maybe she'd be back, maybe not. Maybe she'd find shelter, maybe her therapist or the support group could help, maybe—

Maybe he'd never see her again.

The first sob wracked his frame, and he choked on it. He covered his face with his hands and cried like a baby, standing alone in the dark, in the perfume of grease and diesel.

The stink was overwhelming, but he couldn't cover his nose; it was all he could do to keep forcing the lid up, up, and back without losing his balance in the cramped confines of the pit. He had considered backing the wrecker to the edge of the grave, and using the tow chain the pull the lid off, but no; he was so close, why fuck around? Now he wished he had used the truck. The rain was washing mud and grit into the coffin itself as Michael forced it open further, his back and shoulders screaming with the effort. Finally, he tipped it over, losing his balance as the slippery muck and displaced weight of the damned slab took him down with it.

The lid hit the side of the pit, then threatened to

slide back over the coffin. Michael forced his right leg under it. He had to stop it...

It stopped, hesitating before forcing a broken splinter of bone out of the meat of his lower leg.

For a moment, the pain didn't register, and the face that the coffin lid had stopped sliding was all that mattered to him. Then it shifted again, ever so slightly. He reeled, his hand closing over the jagged tear in his pantleg, shrieking as he tumbled sideways into the coffin.

"Love hurts, love scars, love wounds, and mars..."

The song lilted over the din of the storm, the clanging of the tow chain and creaking of the took belt. His eyes were dry now, dry and burning.

"...a-a-anyone, not tough, grows strong e-nough..."

Michael's fists were taut on the steering wheel, and he drove like a man possessed. He took one hand off the wheel and flexed it, feeling its strength, then the other, never taking his eyes off the road.

"...to take a lot of pain, take a lot of pain..."

He'd been driving for hours, and his gut hurt. He had to piss so bad his eyes were floating, but he'd already decided to wait.

"...love is like a cloud, holds a lot of rain..."

He'd wait until he found Ted's grave.

"...Love hurts..."

The windshield wiper pounded, keeping time with the orchestra as the chorus swelled:

"...Love hurts..."

Michael spilled onto the corpse, and suddenly he was face to face with Ted, dead Ted, sunken oily stinking Ted. The lightning flashed, and he could see the peeled leer, the cratered nose, the sockets cupping rotten, milky fruits. Then, the darkness swallowed all. The coffin had done its job for years, and now that it had been violated, its contents were quickly making up for lost time; the stench was too much to bear any longer, and Michael's stomach puckered and emptied itself.

He struggled to push himself away from the body, but as he did so, his leg sent another bolt of pain across his frame.

Michael shuddered and heaved again. A world of shit, all right. A world of shit in a shitstorm, and he was drowning in it.

Bracing his left arm under his side, he kept his face up out of the vomit and rot that swirled in the ever-deepening water. His throat hurt too much to scream again, and his breathing came harder. His ribs ached terribly: he'd hit the side of the coffin hard as he fell, and may have broken a couple.

An odd calm washed over him then, Shock, he told himself. As it did, his breathing steadied, and the rain slowed, until his breathing and the rain, now muffled to a patter, began to rhythmically mesh with a third sound that came from somewhere in the coffin. It was a soft, wet sound, barely audible, somehow sad and infinitely weary. Michael closed his eyes, trying to separate it from the sprinkling rain, his own breathing and ragged heartbeat.

Yes. It was there. Soft, ever so soft, and ever so sad. It came from within the coffin.

soft

soft

soft

soft

He opened his eyes now, his own pain forgotten. He had pinpointed its source, just beside him. He strained to see in the rippling darkness, but it was no use: everything had merged with the night, including himself.

soft

soft

He stared, nevertheless, and was rewarded with a brief flash from overhead as the tail of the storm spit its last. His eyes widened in horror, and his howl was swallowed by the clap of thunder.

There, in the corpse's skeletal hands, pinioned on its

bony talons, was a little girl's heart.

Though withered and forever cheated, it still beat in the darkness.

SELECTED GRAPHIC ALBUMS FROM ECLIPSE

1. **SABRE** BY DON MCGREGOR AND PAUL GULACY
   (1978) 48 pp, 8 1/2 x 11, b&w
   ❑ 10th Ann. edition trade paperback: 6.95
   ❑ 10th Ann. ed. signed limited cloth: 25.95
2. **THE ROCKETEER** BY DAVE STEVENS
   (1985) 72 pp, 8 1/2 x 11 full colour
   ❑ 2nd printing trade paperback: 8.95
   ❑ 2nd printing clothbound: 20.95
3. **SOMERSET HOLMES** BY BRUCE JONES, APRIL CAMPBELL, AND BRENT ANDERSON
   (1987) 128 pp, 8 1/2 x 11, full colour
   ❑ trade paperback: 15.95
   ❑ clothbound: 25.95
   ❑ clothbound signed limited edition: 36.00
4. **SILVERHEELS** BY BRUCE JONES, SCOTT HAMPTON, AND APRIL CAMPBELL
   (1987) 64 pp, 8 1/2 x 11, full colour
   ❑ trade paperback: 8.95
   ❑ hardbound: 15.95
   ❑ hardbound signed limited edition: 25.95
5. **SCOUT: THE FOUR MONSTERS** BY TIMOTHY TRUMAN AND THOMAS YEATES
   (1988) 136 pp, 7 x 10, full colour
   ❑ trade paperback: 15.95
   ❑ clothbound signed limited edition: 36.00
6. **SCOUT: MOUNT FIRE** BY TIMOTHY TRUMAN
   (1989) 148 pp, 7 x 10, full colour
   ❑ trade paperback: 10.95
   ❑ clothbound signed limited edition: 30.95
7. **TOADSWART D'AMPLESTONE** BY TIM CONRAD
   (1989) 122 pp, 8 1/2 x 11, b&w
   ❑ trade paperback: 13.95
   ❑ clothbound signed limited edition: 36.00
8. **BROUGHT TO LIGHT** BY ALAN MOORE, BILL SIENKIEWICZ, JOYCE BRABNER, THOMAS YEATES, AND PAUL MAVRIDES
   (1988) 80 pp, 8 1/2 x 11, full colour
   ❑ trade paperback: 9.95
   ❑ clothbound: 30.95
9. **MIRACLEMAN: BOOK ONE** BY ALAN MOORE, GARRY LEACH, AND ALAN DAVIS
   (1988) 80 pp, 7 x 10, full colour
   ❑ trade paperback: 10.95
   ❑ clothbound: 30.95
10. **MIRACLEMAN: BOOK TWO** BY ALAN MOORE, ALAN DAVIS, CHUCK BECKUM, RICK VEITCH, ET AL
    (1990) 128 pp, 7 x 10, full colour
    ❑ trade paperback: 13.95
    ❑ clothbound: 30.95
11. **REAL LOVE: THE BEST OF THE SIMON & KIRBY ROMANCE COMICS** EDITED BY RICHARD HOWELL
    (1988) 160 pp, 8 1/2 x 11, b&w
    ❑ trade paperback: 13.95
12. **PIGEONS FROM HELL** BY ROBERT E. HOWARD ADAPTED BY SCOTT HAMPTON
    (1988) 64 pp, 8 1/2 x 11, full colour
    ❑ trade paperback: 8.95
    ❑ clothbound signed limited edition: 30.95
13. **TEENAGED DOPE SLAVES & REFORM SCHOOL GIRLS** EDITED BY DEAN MULLANEY
    (1988) 112 pp, 8 1/2 x 11, b&w
    ❑ trade paperback: 10.95
14. **ARIANE AND BLUEBEARD** BY MAURICE MAETERLINCK ADAPTED BY P. CRAIG RUSSELL
    (1988) 48 pp, 7 x 10, full colour
    ❑ trade paperback: 4.95
    ❑ clothbound signed limited edition: 30.95
15. **KRAZY & IGNATZ** BY GEORGE HERRIMAN
    (1988—1990) 64 pp, 9 x 12, b&w
    Trade paperback: 10.95   Limited. Cloth: 30.95
    ❑ Vol. 1: 1916   ❑ Vol. 1: 1916
    ❑ Vol. 2: 1917   ❑ Vol. 2: 1917
    ❑ Vol. 3: 1918   ❑ Vol. 3: 1918
    ❑ Vol. 4: 1919   ❑ Vol. 4: 1919
    ❑ Vol. 5: 1920   ❑ Vol. 5: 1920
    ❑ Vol. 6: 1921   ❑ Vol. 6: 1921
16. **DR WATCHSTOP: ADVENTURES IN TIME AND SPACE** BY KEN MACKLIN
    (1989) 64 pp, 8 1/2/ x 11, full colour
    ❑ trade paperback: 8.95
    ❑ clothbound signed limited edition: 30.95
17. **TAPPING THE VEIN** BY CLIVE BARKER
    ILLUSTRATED BY CRAIG RUSSELL, SCOTT HAMPTON, KLAUS JANSON, JOHN BOLTON, BO HAMPTON, DENYS COWAN, MICHAEL DAVIS
    (1989-1990) 48 pp each, 7 x 10, full colour
    ❑ Book 1 trade paperback: 7.95
    ❑ Book 2 trade paperback: 7.95
    ❑ Book 3 trade paperback: 7.95
18. **THE HOBBIT** BY J. R. R. TOLKIEN ADAPTED BY CHARLES DIXON AND DAVID WENZEL
    (1990) 152 pp, 7 x 10, full colour
    ❑ trade paperback: 13.95
    ❑ clothbound: 40.95
19. **ALEX TOTH'S ZORRO** BY ALEX TOTH
    (1988) 120 pp, 8 1/2 x 11, b&w
    ❑ Vol. 1 trade paperback: 10.95
    ❑ Vol. 2 trade paperback: 10.95
    ❑ clothbound vols. 1 and 2 signed limited edition, together in one slipcase: 55.00
20. **LARRY MARDER'S BEANWORLD** E/ LARRY MARDER
    (1989) 122 pp, 7 x 10, b&w
    ❑ trade paperback: 10.95
    ❑ clothbound signed limited edition: 30.95
21. **POGO & ALBERT** BY WALT KELLY
    (1989-1990) 64 pp, 8 1/2 x 11, full colour
    Trade paperback: 9.95   Limited. Cloth: 30.95
    ❑ Vol. 1   ❑ Vol. 1
    ❑ Vol. 2   ❑ Vol. 2
    ❑ Vol. 3   ❑ Vol. 3
    ❑ Vol. 4   ❑ Vol. 4
22. **THE RETURN OF VALKYRIE** BY TIM TRUMAN, CHUCK DIXON, TOM YEATES, STAN WOCH & WILL BLYBERG
    (1989) 88 pp, 7 x 10, full colour
    ❑ trade paperback: 10.95
    ❑ clothbound signed limited edition: 30.95
23. **WHAT'S MICHAEL?** BY MIKOTO KOBAYASHI
    (1990) 128 pp, 7 x 10, b&w
    ❑ trade paperback: 10.95
    ❑ clothbound limited edition: 30.95
24. **THE MAGIC FLUTE** ADAPTED BY P. CRAIG RUSSELL FROM THE OPERA BY WOLFGANG AMADEUS MOZART
    (1990) 48 pp. each, 7 x 10, full color
    ❑ Vol. 1 trade paperback: 5.95
    ❑ Vol. 2 trade paperback: 5.95
    ❑ Vol. 3 trade paperback: 5.95

For a complete catalogue of Eclipse graphic albums, books, comics, trading cards, and records, send two first class stamps to:
ECLIPSE BOOKS, P.O. BOX 1099,
FORESTVILLE, CALIFORNIA 95436